Book by David Thompson

Music by John Kander

Lyrics by Fred Ebb

Based on the novel
Love Is Just Around the Corner
by Lester Atwell
Originally adapted by George Abbott

A SAMUEL FRENCH ACTING EDITION

SAMUEL FRENCH

FOUNDED 1830

New York Hollywood London Toronto

SAMUELFRENCH.COM

MUSIC USE NOTE

IMPORTANT BILLING AND CREDIT
REQUIREMENTS

All producers of *FLORA, THE RED MENACE* *must* give credit to the Author of the Play in all programs distributed in connection with performances of the Play, and in all instances in which the title of the Play appears for the purposes of advertising, publicizing or otherwise exploiting the Play and/or a production. The name of the Author *must* appear on a separate line on which no other name appears, immediately following the title and *must* appear in size of type not less than fifty percent of the size of the title type.

In addition the following credit *must* be given in all programs and publicity information distributed in association with this piece:

(Name of Producer)
presents

FLORA, THE RED MENACE

Book by	Music by	Lyrics by
David Thompson	John Kander	Fred Ebb

Based on the novel
"Love Is Just Around The Corner" by Lester Atwell

Originally adapted by George Abbott

Vineyard Theatre
Doug Aibel, Artistic Director – Theatre
Barbara Zinn Krieger, Executive Director
Gary P. Steuer, Managing Director
presents

A Musical

Book by	Music by	Lyrics by
DAVID THOMPSON	JOHN KANDER	FRED EBB

based on the novel
"Love Is Just Around The Corner" by Lester Atwell
originally adapted by George Abbott

with

Veanne Cox	Maggy Gorrill	Eddie Korbich
Ray DeMattis	Lyn Greene	Dirk Lumbard
Peter Frechette	B.J. Jefferson	David Ossian

Musical Direction by DAVID POGUE

Scenic design by MICHAEL J. HOTOPP

Lighting design by PHIL MONAT

Costume design by LINDSAY W. DAVIS

Sound design by PHIL LEE

Production Stage Manager MARY FRAN LOFTUS

Choreography by SUSAN STROMAN

Directed by SCOTT ELLIS

FLORA, THE RED MENACE was presented by the Vineyard Theater, 309 East 26th, Doug Aibel, Artistic Director, Barbara Zinn Krieger, Executive Director, Gary P. Steuer, Managing Director for a limited run November 20 to January 23, 1988.

FLORA MESZAROS	Veanne Cox
HARRY TOUKARIAN	Peter Frechette
CHARLOTTE	Lyn Greene
WILLY AND OTHERS	Eddie Korbich
MR. WEISS AND OTHERS	Ray DeMattis
ELSA AND OTHERS	B.J. Jefferson
KENNY AND OTHERS	Dirk Lumbard
MAGGIE AND OTHERS	Maggy Gorrill
MR. STANLEY AND OTHERS	David Ossian

Directed by Scott Ellis
Choreography by Susan Stroman
Scenic Design by Michael J. Hotopp
Lighting by Phil Monat
Costumes by Lindsay W. Davis
Sound by Phil Lee
Musical Direction by David Pogue
Production Stage Manager Mary Fran Loftus

CAST

FLORA MESZAROS

HARRY TOUKARIAN

CHARLOTTE

WILLY
  —Sam, an artist
  —Communist
  —Elevator Operator

MR. WEISS
  —Apple seller on street
  —Galka, Communist leader
  —Man on elevator with newspaper

ELSA
  —Office runner
  —Esther, a Communist
  —Woman on elevator

MAGGIE
  —Secretary, Miss Williams
  —Darla, a Communist

KENNY
  —Bob, an artist
  —Patrick, a Communist

MR. STANLEY
  —Pete, an artist
  —Toby, a Communist

CHARACTER DESCRIPTIONS

FLORA MESZAROS
A young fashion illustrator, full of hope, optimism and the desire to take over the world. She is absolutely guileless, willing to take on any challenge, without a trace of brassiness.

HARRY TOUKARIAN
A shy, intense, oddly handsome artist. He stammers— especially when he is nervous. He has a romantic vision of how to make society perfect.

CHARLOTTE
A bit of a misfit, a party zealot, she is determined to spread Communism singlehandedly. She is dry, droll—the quintessential comic villian.

WILLY
Very boyish, spirited. A songwriter who plays the clarinet, Willy, in a sense, serves as the narrator for the play.

ELSA
Extremely practical, pulled together, she has aspirations to be a fashion designer and has yet to get up the nerve to get her sketches around town.

MR. WEISS
A former Communist who has lost his jewelery shop to the Depression, he is kindly, knowing.

MAGGIE
Very innocent. Honest. Maggie came to New York from Oklahoma following a dust storm. She is now trying to get a break with her dance partner, Kenny.

KENNY
Moving with Ray Bolger-like limberness and comedy, he is very serious about his dancing and determined to get ahead.

MR. STANLEY
Arrow Shirt Collar-perfect. The perfect department store executive. Easily disliked.

A NOTE ABOUT THE SET

The set for the play should be as simple as possible. The space should have the feeling of a rehearsal hall in 1935 with actors entering from several different points, including the audience. All the needed furniture for the different scenes can be suggested with assorted chairs, crates, planks and the like. A simple table can be used as Flora's work desk, the Communist Party podium, Mr. Stanley's desk. Harry's room can be suggested by a free-standing door unit and a metal framed cot.

Different set dressing—perhaps a window card at Garret and Mellick's with winter fashions, a billboard in the park, a banner in the Communist Party meeting, a window drape in the studio—can be brought on for color. All set changes should be done in full view of the audience and done by the cast members. This is a WPA production and everyone plays their part. They run spotlights, work the snow-trough, carry on props.

Much of the mood is created through lighting. Wall sconces are used to suggest the studio, street lamps to create the outside, hanging lamps to contribute to the overall effect of the Communist Party meeting. Costumes should be kept simple and—with the exception of the gowns—look like street clothes from the period. The piano may be onstage in full view of the audience.

Most importantly, to create the illusion of this being a WPA project, enormous murals—done in the style of Thomas Hart Benton—should hang on the walls of the theater. They should show scenes of life in New York in the Thirties and reflect the dreams, struggles and realities of the common man.

NEW YORK CITY 1935

ACT ONE

9

ACT TWO

10

PROLOGUE

(*As the audience enters the theater, an onstage radio plays music, commercials and skits from a 1935 radio show.*
WILLY comes onstage, turns off the radio and addresses the audience.)

WILLY. Good evening. And welcome. We're really glad you made it here tonight.

Well, it's been a tough year — 1935 — I don't have to tell you that. But we're really excited because through the Federal Theater Project, we are able to present this production to you tonight.

I would like to point out that there are nine of us to play twenty-five parts — so — until the economy turns around, we're going to have to ask you to use your imagination.

(*Nodding to the stage manager.*) I see we're ready to begin. We hope you enjoy FLORA, THE RED MENACE.

(*He exits as the lights dim and the opening number begins.*)

11

ACT ONE

SCENE ONE

(The entire ensemble, with the exception of Flora, is onstage.
It is the height of the Depression. They wear winter overcoats and
*   try to keep out the cold.*
Each one of the speeches is done brightly, without a hint of de-
*   spair. Despite the economic forecast, there is a sense of opti-*
*   mism and hope.)*

[MUSIC #1 *PROLOGUE*]

ACTOR #1.
APPLES
  ACTOR #2.
PENCILS
  ACTOR #1/#2.
ONLY A NICKEL, MISTER
  ACTOR #2.
PENCILS
  ACTOR #1.
APPLES
  ACTOR #1/#2.
ONLY A NICKEL, MISTER
  ACTOR #3. Have one dish every week that's a complete sur-
prise. That's what the magazine says. Who are they kidding?
Every time we HAVE a dish it's a surprise.
  ACTOR #4. Things are tough. The soles on my shoes are so thin
I could stand on a dime and tell you if it were heads . . . or tails.
  ACTOR #5/#6/#7.
I DON'T WANT YOUR SISTER
I DON'T WANT YOUR WIFE
MISTER JUST GIVE ME A JOB

I DON'T WANT YOUR BUICK
THE GLORY OF YOUR LIFE
MISTER JUST GIVE ME A JOB
  ACTOR #5. So. We had a strike. I said to the girls, 'Just sit, don't
do nothin'.' So we sat around. We joked about a lot of things. Had

a lot of fun. But the boss. He went crazy. He called us a bunch of Communists. The girls didn't even know what he meant.

ACTOR #8. Said Billy Rose to Sally Rand, "Can you do your act without your fan?" Sally Rand dropped her fan. Billy Rose. Sally Rand.

ALL.

I DON'T NEED YOUR
  SWEEPER
TO KEEP MY CASTLE
  CLEAN
MISTER JUST GIVE ME A
  JOB

CANCEL MY
  SUBSCRIPTION
TO FORTUNE MAGAZINE
MISTER JUST GIVE ME A
  JOB

OO BABA
DO WAH OO CLEAN OH,
MISTER JUST GIVE ME A
  JOB

BUNG BUNG
BUNG BUNG
MISTER JUST GIVE ME A
  JOB

ACTOR #6. Behind the counters, girls are making twenty-five cents an hour. Coolie wages. Oh, a worker's got no right to have kids anymore.

ACTOR #2. At New York department stores, to run an elevator, you need a college diploma.

ACTOR #1. I read the other day everything's under control. The politicians say "Don't worry . . . there'll never be another crash."

ALL.

MELLON PULLED THE WHISTLE
HOOVER RANG THE BELL
WALL STREET GAVE THE SIGNAL
AND THE COUNTRY WENT TO HELL

(*Everyone exits except for Willy.*)

WILLY. Ladies and gentlemen, valedictorian of the graduating class, Miss Flora Meszaros.

(*There is applause from the wings. Flora rushes on. She is late. She smiles as she passes and then steps up onto a crate. Willy motions to her to straighten her mortar board. She does. She collects her thoughts and then begins with determination.*)

FLORA. Members of the faculty, fellow graduates and honored

guests. We stand on the threshold of the future. We, the youth of the nation, have a responsibility. A mission. And I would like to say in the words of our great president . . .

[MUSIC #2 *OPENING (UNAFRAID)*]

(*spoken*)
We have nothing to fear
We will not be afraid
Eyes unclouded and clear
We will join the great parade.

(*singing*)
PROUDLY MARCHING ALONG
TOWARD A SUNNIER DAY
FIERCE, DETERMINED AND STRONG
EVER READY COME WHAT MAY
BRUISED AND BATTERED
BUT WE WILL BE UNBOWED
CLOUDS MAY GATHER AND SWARM
YET, THIS PROMISE IS MADE
WE WILL WEATHER THE STORM
UNIFORMLY UNAFRAID

Will you all please rise and take this oath with me? I will give you the words. "We have nothing to fear." (*The graduates enter, wearing caps and gowns.*)
  GRADUATES.
WE HAVE NOTHING TO FEAR
  FLORA. "We will not be afraid."
  GRADUATES.
WE WILL NOT BE AFRAID
  FLORA. "Eyes unclouded and clear."
  GRADUATES.
EYES UNCLOUDED AND CLEAR
  FLORA. "We will join the great parade.
  ALL.
WE WILL JOIN THE GREAT PARADE
PROUDLY MARCHING ALONG
TOWARD A SUNNIER DAY
FIERCE DETERMINED AND STRONG
EVER READY COME WHAT MAY

BRUISED AND BATTERED
BUT WE WILL BE UNBOWED
CLOUDS MAY GATHER AND SWARM
YET, THIS PROMISE IS MADE
WE WILL WEATHER THE STORM
UNIFORMLY UNAFRAID
UNCONDITIONALLY
UNAFRAID!

(A flashbulb pops and catches the moment. During the following musical transition, the actors take off their caps and gowns and change the scene to Garret and Mellick's, a department store.)

[MUSIC #2a *"MISTER JOB" (SCENE CHANGE)*]

WILLY.
I DON'T NEED YOUR CHAUFFEUR
TO DRIVE ME INTO TOWN
MISTER JUST GIVE ME A JOB

DON'T NEED YOUR DIPLOMA
OR YOUR CAP AND GOWN
MISTER JUST GIVE ME A JOB
   ALL.
MISTER JUST GIVE ME A JOB

SCENE TWO

A waiting room at Garret and Mellick's.
(Three artists are seated, filling out job applications. They have illustration design samples ready to turn in.
An attractive secretary, wearing a polka-dotted dress, sits at a desk.
Also seated is Harry Toukarian, a shy, intense and oddly handsome artist. He seems out of place and quietly reads a book.
Flora enters. She carries her oversized carpetbag.)
   FLORA. Well! Whaddya know. A reunion. (*The artists warmly greet her.*) Or should I call this our very own breadline. Gimbel's, Sak's, Macy's, Altman's—and now the great Garret and Mellick's.
   SECRETARY. Please take a seat.

FLORA. Only the best waiting rooms for the up and coming—
SAM. Unemployed.

FLORA. Thank you—fashion illustrators of America. Any truth to the rumor of a job opening?

PETE. We're waiting to see if Mr. Stanley will even look at our samples.

FLORA. Oh.

BOB. Get an application.

FLORA. Alright. (*She goes to take an application. The secretary puts her hand on top of the stack.*)

SECRETARY. I don't know what good it's going to do you. (*Then she hands Flora an application.*)

FLORA. (*Ignoring the haughtiness of the secretary.*) Thank you. (*Seeing Harry.*) Hey! A new face. (*She sits next to him.*)

HARRY. Wha—ah—me?

FLORA. Ya, you. I'm Flora Meszaros. Hungarian. (*She puts out her hand.*)

HARRY. Oh—uh—Harry Toukarian. Armenian. (*A little confused, he shakes her hand.*)

FLORA. Well, whaddya know. A couple of foreigners. I've never seen you in these parts. Are you an illustrator?

HARRY. Well—uh—I—I—I

FLORA. Sometimes I'm not so sure myself.

RUNNER. (*Entering with merchandise.*) This is the merchandise for Mr. Stanley.

SECRETARY. Say—you know you're supposed to use the back door. I have told you that a dozen times. (*The runner begins to back up.*)

HARRY. (*Standing up.*) No! You sh-should go out the same way you c-came in. You're a human b-being. It's your right. (*The runner exits the way she came in. The secretary bristles. Everyone in the office except Flora is uncomfortable. Harry sits down. Flora looks at him. She is impressed.*)

FLORA. Gee! (*As she turns to fill out the job application, she very subtly begins flirting with Harry.*)

[MUSIC #2b *LAST NAME*]

FLORA.
LAST NAME, PLEASE PRINT PLAINLY
MESZAROS
M-E-S-Z-A-R-O-S

FIRST NAME, PLEASE PRINT PLAINLY
FLORA . . . THAT MEANS FLOWER
HOME ADDRESS . . . 307 WEST FOURTH
GET OFF AT SHERIDAN SQUARE
WALK NORTH
PREVIOUS EXPERIENCE . . . NONE
REASON FOR APPLYING FOR THIS POSITION . . .
REASON FOR APPLYING FOR THIS POSITION?!
(*Grandly*) WELL IT GOT SO BORING IN THE PENTHOUSE
WITH NO ONE BUT THE SERVANTS AROUND
I THOUGHT I'D TAKE A JOB AMONG THE PEOPLE
THEY'RE ALWAYS SO AMUSING I HAVE FOUND

(*The telephone rings. The secretary answers it.*)

[MUSIC #2c *SECRETARY UNDERSCORE*]

Oh, this is rich. The trick to these situations is never to be caught DEAD waiting in a waiting room. (*Flora gets up and goes over to the secretary. As she passes the artists she says under her breath*) Get out your samples.

    SECRETARY. (*Hanging up the phone.*) THAT was Mr. Stanley.
    FLORA. Your dress — it's part of the new cruise line, isn't it?
    SECRETARY. He's not accepting any design samples today. There are NO jobs.
    FLORA. Did I say anything about jobs? I did not. I just said that's a darling dress. Come on. Turn around. (*A little warily, the secretary does.*) Boys, doesn't this dress make you feel like a quick game of shuffle board?
    ARTISTS. (*They hoot and whistle. The secretary spins around. She is furious.*)
    SECRETARY. THAT will be enough. You'll have to leave — (*she returns to her seat.*)
    FLORA. Apparently madame, it's escaped your attention. See here. (*She shows the secretary the application.*) Do you know who I am? (*Then to Harry.*) Can you believe this, Harry? She doesn't know who *I* am.

[MUSIC #3 *THE KID HERSELF*]

    FLORA. (*To secretary.*)
STEP RIGHT UP

AND MEET THE KID HERSELF
THE MOST IMPRESSIVE SIGHT
IN ALL OF NEW YORK CITY
SHE CAN DO
WHAT VERY FEW CAN DO
(SHE EVEN TALKS HUNGARIAN)

(*The secretary leaves. Through the following verse, Flora gathers
    up the artwork from the other artists and then puts the sam-
    ples into the box of merchandise on the secretary's desk.*)

STEP RIGHT UP
AND YOU WILL ANSWER "YES"
THE WONDERS OF THE WORLD
ARE REALLY EIGHT, NOT SEVEN
ON THE LIST
BESIDE THE PYRAMID
YOU GOTTA PUT
THE KID HERSELF

(*She sits next to Harry. He smiles and quickly returns to his book.
    She begins in earnest to try and get his attention.*)

THE KID HERSELF
GOES ANY PLACE
AND FELLAS FOLLOW HER LIKE CATTLE
LOOK AT THE FORM
LOOK AT THE FACE
NOW DON'T THEY MAKE YOUR BACK TEETH
  RATTLE?

ON TOP OF WHICH
SHE'S FILTHY RICH
SHE SELLS HER SKETCHES BY THE GROSS
WHICH ONLY GOES TO SHOW
WHAT YOU'VE BEEN MISSING, JOE
IF YOU HAVE MISSED
MISS MESZ-AR-OS
SO KINDLY . . .

STEP RIGHT UP
AND MEET THE KID HERSELF

THE MOST AMAZING MISS
IN ALL OF NEW YORK CITY
SHE HAS GOT
WHAT VERY FEW HAVE GOT
(YOU OUGHTA SEE HER STUDIO!)

STEP RIGHT UP
AND YOU WILL CAST YOUR VOTE
OUTSIDE IN BRYANT PARK
THEY OUGHT TO PUT A STATUE
THERE SHE IS
SO KINDLY DOFF YOUR LID
IN HONOR OF
THE KID HERSELF
THE KID HERSELF
 ARTISTS.
THE KID HERSELF
 FLORA.
TOOK HER I.Q.
 ARTISTS.
TOOK HER I.Q.
 FLORA.
AND HER PROFESSORS WERE ASTOUNDED
THAT GORGEOUS THING
 ARTISTS.
THAT GORGEOUS THING
 FLORA.
IS BRAINY TOO
 ARTISTS.
SHE'S BRAINY TOO
 FLORA.
WHEN WAS A LADY SO WELL ROUNDED?
PLUS SHE CAN COOK
 ARTISTS.
PLUS SHE CAN COOK
 FLORA.
DON'T OVERLOOK
 ARTISTS.
DON'T OVERLOOK
 FLORA.
NO OTHER GOULASH CAN COME CLOSE

YES, SHE'S A TRIPLE THREAT
YOU AIN'T SEEN NOTHIN' YET
TIL YOU HAVE MET
MISS MESZ-AR-OS
  ARTISTS.
THE KID HERSELF
  FLORA. Who can that be?
  ARTISTS.
HAS SO MUCH POISE
  FLORA. They must mean me.
  ARTISTS.
ON HER A PERSIAN LAMB LOOKS SABLE
  FLORA. Sable!
  ARTISTS.
THE PRINCE OF WALES
  FLORA. I knock him dead.
  ARTISTS.
WHOM SHE DESTROYS
  FLORA. I call him Ed.
  ARTISTS.
PROPOSES TWICE A DAY BY CABLE
  FLORA. Cable!
  ARTISTS.
AWAY OUT WEST
  FLORA. Away out west.
  ARTISTS.
AT MGM
  FLORA. You heard of them?
  ARTISTS.
LOUIS B. MAYER'S ON THE PHONE
  FLORA.
TO HOLLER "FLORA DEAR
PLEASE HURRY UP OUT HERE
  ARTISTS.
WE WANT TO STAR THE KID HERSELF
  FLORA.
WITH GABLE."
  FLORA/ARTISTS.
LA LA LA LA LA LA LA
LA LA
LA LA LA LA LA LA
LA LA LA LA LA LA LA

FLORA.
(*SHE WAS A VALEDICTORY*)
ARTISTS.
LA DI DA DI DA DI
LA DI DA DI DA DI
ON THE LIST BESIDE THE PYRAMID
FLORA.
BESIDE THE HANGING GARDENS
ARTISTS.
AND THE COLOSSUS OF RHODES
FLORA.
AND . .
AND THE OTHER FOUR
YOU GOTTA PUT THE KID HERSELF
ARTISTS.
THE KID HERSELF
HARRY. (*He drops his book. He wasn't expecting any of this.*)
Gee!
ARTISTS.
THE KID HERSELF
HAS SO MUCH CLASS
AND SUCH AN ELEGANT DEMEANOR
THE OTHER GIRLS
WHO SEE HER PASS
CAN FEEL THEIR FACES GROWING GREENER
PROCEED AT WILL
HER LOOK CAN KILL
YOU MUSTN'T TAKE A LETHAL DOSE
FLORA.
ALTHOUGH YOU MIGHT REPLY
"WHAT BETTER WAY TO DIE
FLORA/ARTISTS.
THAN IN THE ARMS
OF FLORA MESZAROS!"
THE KID HERSELF
FLORA. And THAT'S who I am! (*The secretary returns.*)
SECRETARY. You're all going to have to leave. That means
you, Miss Budapest. (*She returns to her desk.*)
HARRY. Awww—l-lady. Don't b-b-bust a gasket. The
woman's just t-trying to get a j-job.
FLORA. Why—thank you.

HARRY. (*There is an awkward moment.*) You're
—you're—welcome.

SECRETARY. Will you please leave?!

ARTISTS. (*They begin to get up and gather their things.*) Alright!
Okay.

FLORA. (*Harry begins to go.*) Hey, hey, hey—don't go. Hey!
Where are you going? Hey!

HARRY. Me?

FLORA. Yes, you—Harry.

HARRY. I've g-got an appointment.

FLORA. You've got time for a quick cup of coffee, don't you?

HARRY. With you.

FLORA. No. (*Refering to secretary.*) With her. Yes with me!

HARRY. Now?

FLORA. Now.

SECRETARY. NOW!

HARRY. I—I—I—uh

FLORA. I'll take that as a yes. (*To secretary.*) We're leaving.

SECRETARY. Good! (*The secretary leaves and takes the box of
merchandise with the samples inside into Mr. Stanley's office.*)

FLORA. (*Calling out to her.*) Tell Mr. Stanley to give me a ring.
And that dress! (*To the artists.*) I wouldn't wear it to a shipwreck!
(*She exits.*)

[MUSIC #3a "KID" PLAYOFF/APPLES]

SCENE THREE

On the street, moments later

[MUSIC #3a APPLES (CON'T)]

APPLE SELLER. (*As the scene changes.*)
APPLES, APPLES
ONLY A NICKEL MISTER

HARRY. (*Entering, carrying his portfolio. He buys an apple.*)
Mister, an apple.

APPLE SELLER. Thanks, buddy.

HARRY. Sure thing. (*The apple seller exits.*)

FLORA. (*She rushes after him.*) Harry, that is the third secretary
and the third waiting room I've dealt with today. Sometimes I
think they must figure we've got nothing better to do than just sit
around. Isn't that true?

HARRY. Ya—uh—I—I

FLORA. I mean by the end of the day, I feel like a piece of furniture. Do you?

HARRY. Oh—I—uh

FLORA. Do I look like a piece of furniture?

HARRY. No.

FLORA. (*Momentarily at a loss for words.*) That's a SWELL hat you have on.

HARRY. Th-th-th

FLORA. Thank you?

HARRY. Thank you. I stammer.

FLORA. Oh. Who would notice! Not me!

HARRY. That's very nice of you to s-say that.

FLORA. (*Determined to continue the conversation.*) So Harry . . . you're an artist.

HARRY. Oh—well—(*He steps away.*)

FLORA. Well me too. At least I try to be. The last job I drew ads for a paper in Bayside. The Daily Journal. Do you know it?

HARRY. No.

FLORA. Well, the publisher didn't have any money so he used the barter system. Which would have been okay—but he owned a cemetary. I quit at seven plots.

HARRY. (*This touches something in him.*) You should have stood up for your rights. Organized a s-strike!

FLORA. (*He's finally talking.*) A strike?

HARRY. Yeah!

FLORA. Sure! A strike! (*She doesn't know what he is talking about.*)

HARRY. And g-gotten your money.

FLORA. Of course he didn't have any money.

HARRY. So—you could have g-gotten s-something.

FLORA. Right! Maybe more cemetary plots. I could have buried my whole family in a month.

HARRY. But something.

FLORA. Sure. (*She sees the point.*)

HARRY. You have to fight for what's fair.

FLORA. (*She becomes increasingly more determined and animated.*) Yeah! That's right. (*She swings her arms in the air, shadowboxing the world.*) No more cemetary plots!

HARRY. A-a-absolutely.

FLORA. No more waiting rooms. (*She swings her arms even more aggressively.*)

HARRY. Ya s-see that?

FLORA. No more polka-dotted SECRETARIES! (*She swings around and punches Harry right in the nose.*) Oh my god!

HARRY. Woah! Put those plots of yours to g-good use.

FLORA. Oh! I'm so sorry.

HARRY. It's not the first time.

FLORA. Look—we can get some ice at my studio. (*She goes through her bag to get a handkerchief.*)

HARRY. No! No! No, no, no. We don't have to g-g-go to your s-studio.

FLORA. It's just around the corner.

HARRY. No! I'm—ah—just fine. I'll j-just go on my way.

FLORA. (*She will not give in.*) Harry! Please. I insist. (*She picks up Harry's portfolio and book.*)

HARRY. Uh—I—uh

FLORA. "My studio." Doesn't that sound grand? It's nothing really. I mean, it IS something. But not THAT much something. It's just an old ballroom in the Hotel Sedgewick.

HARRY. Listen—

FLORA. I rent it out to different artists and at the end of the month—if everything comes out right—I make a little money.

HARRY. The collective cause.

FLORA. Of course, nothing has come out right. Yet. But it will. One of us has got to make some money. I mean, we're an odd bunch. [MUSIC #4 *ONE GOOD BREAK*] But we're kinda like family. We might as well be—we practically LIVE in the studio. First off, there's Kenny and Maggie . . .

(*Harry and Flora start to exit as Maggie comes onto the stage. Maggie flips a light switch and the wall sconces in the studio come on. She has just come in from outside and takes off her coat. Flora and Maggie's dialogue overlap. The underscoring for the song begins. Each of the speeches incorporated into the song is delivered directly to the audience.*)

FLORA. Maggie ran a dance studio in Oklahoma until . . .

SCENE FOUR

The Studio

MAGGIE. (*overlapping with Flora's dialogue.*) I ran a dance studio in Oklahoma until one afternoon the whole place just blew away. So I came to New York. That first afternoon, I went to this automat—you know—the one on 57th Street. And there was Flora. She was going from table to table asking every woman there if she wanted to go on this blind date with this guy. (*Kenny enters. He takes off his coat.*) It was Kenny. When she got to me—well—I don't know why but for some reason I said yes. Only it turned out, it wasn't a regular blind date. Oh no! It was a dance marathon.

KENNY. Thirteen days and nights I danced with this girl—Maggie—I didn't even know. Just to stay awake we told each other the most amazing things about ourselves. And you know what? We lost. But we discovered we made a damn good dance team. A damn good one. Flora rented us space in her studio and now all we need is for someone to give us an audition. (*Maggie hands him his dance shoes as they are about ready to rehearse.*)

[MUSIC #4: *ALL I NEED IS ONE GOOD BREAK*]

KENNY.
ALL I NEED IS ONE GOOD BREAK
JUST ONE GOOD BREAK
THEN MISTER WATCH MY SPEED
MAGGIE.
ALL I NEED IS ONE GOOD BREAK JUST ONE
KENNY.
ONE SUBSTANTIAL BREAK IS ALL I NEED
MAGGIE.
ONE SUBSTANTIAL BREAK IS ALL I NEED
TO MAKE THEM ALL STAND UP AND CHEER
KENNY. (*Counterpoint.*)
ONE SUBSTANTIAL BREAK IS ALL I NEED
TO MAKE THEM ALL STAND UP AND CHEER
MAGGIE.
I COULD SET THIS TOWN RIGHT ON ITS EAR
KENNY.
I COULD SET THIS TOWN RIGHT ON ITS EAR
GIMME GIMME A CHANCE
MAGGIE.
GIMME GIMME A CHANCE
KENNY/MAGGIE.
I DON'T WANT ANY HANDOUT
GIMME GIMME A BOOST

AND I'LL NEVER BE FANNED OUT
GIMME GIMME A LIFT
 MAGGIE.
AND REPORTERS WILL STAND OUTSIDE MY DOOR
ALL BEGGING FOR THE CHANCE TO GET AN
 EXCLUSIVE

(*Willy enters from outside. He carries his clarinet case. As he takes off his coat, he greets Kenny and Maggie.*)

 KENNY/MAGGIE.
ALL I NEED IS ONE GOOD BREAK
JUST ONE GOOD BREAK THEN MISTER WATCH
 MY SPEED
ONE SUBSTANTIAL BREAK IS ALL I NEED

 WILLY. (*About their dancing.*) Hey, pretty good. (*To the audience.*) My name is Willy. I've been trying to get into a band around town. Times are tough. Which is just my luck. I met Flora one day when I was playing my clarinet in the park. She thought I was . . . great. She told me about a dance team that needed some new material for their act. So I rented space in the studio — wrote them a song — and haven't made a penny. Which is just my luck. (*Elsa enters from the outside. She takes off her coat.*) But one thing that keeps me going. Women can't get enough of a man who plays the clarinet. (*Elsa kisses Willy on the cheek.*) Which, thank god, is just my luck.

 ELSA. (*To the audience.*) Hi. I'm Elsa. Flora and I have been best girlfriends since . . . just about forever. (*She holds up a dress she has been working on.*) Tell me. Do you like this dress? You could get a lot of use out of it — no? You could dress it up, dress it down. I'm very good at putting things together. Flora says I should start showing my designs around town. Maybe I will. Like Eleanor Roosevelt says, "You don't get anywhere by standing still."

 ELSA.
GIMME GIMME A CHANCE
 WILLY.
GIMME GIMME A CHANCE
 ELSA/WILLY.
AND I'M OFF TO THE BIG TIME
GIMME GIMME A BOOST
AND I'LL MAKE IT IN JIG TIME

GIMME GIMME A LIFT
ELSA.
AND I'LL WAGER A FIG TIME MAGAZINE
WILL ASK FOR ME TO BE THE FACE ON THE COVER
ELSA/WILLY.
ALL I NEED IS ONE GOOD BREAK
JUST ONE GOOD BREAK THEN MISTER WATCH
  MY SPEED

(*Willy plays the melody on the clarinet.*)

MR. WEISS. (*Mr. Weiss enters. He has been fixing a watch and wears a jeweler's magnifying glass.*) Weiss. Julius Weiss. Perhaps you knew my shop. One-Nine-Eight Sixth Avenue. Fine jewelry. For all occasions. Except a Depression. The shop — it will reopen soon. And in the meantime? I rent space from Flora and I fix watches. Enough to eat. Enough for a cup of coffee with my young friends here. So full of hope. Poor deluded fools you say? I say it's a good sign that this terrible depression has not killed the spirit of the young.
KENNY/MAGGIE/WILLY/ELSA.
GIMME GIMME A CHANCE
AND I KNOW I CAN DO IT
GIMME GIMME A BOOST
AND I'M GOING TO SEE TO IT
GIMME GIMME A LIFT AND
WILLY.
I'LL BUY ME SOME NEW ITALIAN CLOTHES
MAGGIE.
SOME FRENCH PERFUME
KENNY.
AND STRIKE A FANCY POSE
ELSA.
AND ELEVATE MY NOSE
ALL.
AND MOM AND DAD WOULDN'T KNOW ME
ALL I NEED IS ONE GOOD BREAK
JUST ONE GOOD BREAK
AND MISTER WATCH MY SPEED
ONE SUBSTANTIAL BREAK IS ALL I NEED
KENNY/MAGGIE.
ONE SUBSTANTIAL BREAK IS ALL I NEED

WILLY/ELSA.
ONE SUBSTANTIAL BREAK IS ALL I NEED
    MR. WEISS.
ALL I NEED IS ONE GOOD BREAK

(*Willy plays his clarinet again*)

    ALL.
ONE!

(*Everyone returns to work. Flora enters with Harry who still holds a handkerchief on his nose.*)

FLORA. Hello, everyone! (*The artists greet Flora.*) I'd like you to meet Harry Toukarian. This is Mr. Weiss—
MR. WEISS. A pleasure.
FLORA. Elsa
ELSA. Hi.
FLORA. Willy.
WILLY. Willy—hi.
FLORA. Kenny and Maggie.
MAGGIE. Nice to meet you.
FLORA. My family. (*Flora pulls up a chair for Harry.*)
ELSA. And not one of us Hungarian.
FLORA. Willy, will you get some ice?
WILLY. And some glasses.
ELSA. Cocktails!
WILLY. And some mixers!
FLORA. No! Just ice. It's for his nose. (*Willy exits. Harry sits as the artists gather around him.*)
MAGGIE. What happened? (*She looks at Flora.*) You hit him?
FLORA. It was an accident.
KENNY. Some accident.
FLORA. Harry's a fashion illustrator.
KENNY. A fashion illustrator?
HARRY. Well ac-ac-actually—I'm not.
FLORA. Like I said. (*Flora takes off her coat and hangs it up.*)
HARRY. No-I've n-never done it.
KENNY. You're kidding.
HARRY. No.
MR. WEISS. Then what were you doing there? (*The artists lean in a bit.*)

HARRY. I-I-I-wh—I-I-I (*He is getting a little nervous.*) I was trying to g-g-get . . . (*The artists continue to lean.*) . . . a j . . . (*finally*) a job. I stammer.

ELSA. Willy, where's that ice?

WILLY. (*Entering.*) I got it. (*Elsa takes it and carefully puts it onto Harry's nose.*)

HARRY. I mean, I do paint.

MAGGIE. Oh! What do you paint?

HARRY. I used to paint subways.

KENNY. Subways?

HARRY. C-Ceilings. Public Works.

ELSA. Ah—the modern day Sistine Chapel.

MAGGIE. So are you going to rent space? (*The artists all begin talking at once about the studio. Flora realizes she is standing on the sidelines.*)

FLORA.   Everyone—Please!   He's—He's—convalescing. Right Harry? (*She takes the ice from Elsa.*)

HARRY. Uh-oh-I

FLORA. Right. (*Flora puts the ice on Harry's nose. Everyone leans in a bit closer. Flora looks up and smiles—letting them know they should all get lost. Kenny and Maggie catch on. So does Elsa.*)

KENNY. Uh Maggie—we gotta go to—uh—work.

MAGGIE. Nice to meet you Harry.

ELSA. (*She whispers into Flora's ear and then giggles.*)

FLORA. (*Willy continues to stare at Harry.*) Willy!

WILLY. Huh? Oh, yeah—okay. (*He leaves.*)

FLORA. (*And finally*) Mr. Weiss. (*He smiles and leaves. Absent-mindedly, she puts the ice on Harry's nose a little carelessly. Harry winces.*) Oh! I'm sorry!

HARRY. It's like you have your own community here. (*Flora is very touched.*) It's v-v-very impressive.

FLORA. Thanks.

HARRY. (*Then.*) Look, F-Flora—I have to g-go.(*He begins to get up.*)

FLORA. Go! Aw, you just got here. (*Thinking fast.*) I want to see your portfolio. (*She grabs it.*)

HARRY. I've got to get to an—

FLORA. (*Taking portfolio.*) An appointment. I know. Gosh. I haven't heard that word in such a long time. It sounds so . . . grand. "An appointment." Let me guess. A job interview.

HARRY. N-no. Nothing like that.

FLORA. A social function?

HARRY. No.

FLORA. A woman?

HARRY. (*Embarrassed.*) No.

FLORA. Good. (*She opens his portfolio and flips through a few pages. Harry is embarrassed and a little nervous. He turns away.*) Harry . . . your work is really great.

HARRY. Oh—you d-don't have to say that.

FLORA. No, really—it is!

HARRY. You think so?

FLORA. Look, I know what's good and this is good.

HARRY. Well-I-uh—I've been working at it.

FLORA. Listen, Harry—there's space here in the studio. Why don't you paint here?

HARRY. Uh-well-uh-oh-thanks. But I don't have any m-money right now.

FLORA. Why let a little thing like money get in your way.

HARRY. Well—

FLORA. Look—pay me what you can. Everybody else does. You're not going to be in this boat forever.

HARRY. No—r-really—I d-d-don't have anything.

FLORA. You've got an apple don't you?

HARRY. What—this? (*He takes the apple out of his pocket.*)

FLORA. Pay me in apples.

HARRY. Aw, no—I couldn't do that.

FLORA. Sure you could.

HARRY. That's very very nice of you—the ice—the—

FLORA. Then it's a deal?

HARRY. It's—it's—it's

FLORA. It's a deal. [MUSIC #5 *NOT EVERY DAY OF THE WEEK*] (*She takes the apple.*) Besides. Who knows what an apple might lead to.

[MUSIC #5: *IT'S NOT EVERY DAY OF THE WEEK*]

HARRY.
YOU'RE VERY AGGRESSIVE
(*IN THE NICEST WAY POSSIBLE*)
I MEAN THAT YOU'RE PUSHY
(*THAT IS TO SAY BOLD*)
I FEEL LIKE I'VE BEEN RUN OVER

(*IN THE NICEST WAY POSSIBLE*)
AND BELIEVE ME, WHATEVER YOU'RE SELLING
I'M SOLD

THE MOMENT I SAW YOU
I KNEW LIKE A SHOT
YOU WERE VERY DISTINCTIVE, AND
I HAVE TO ACKNOWLEDGE

IT'S NOT EVERY DAY OF THE WEEK
AND NOT EVERY WEEK OF THE YEAR
THAT SOMEONE AS AVERAGE AS EVERDAY ME
MEETS SOMEONE SO SPECIAL SO
IF I'M TONGUE-TIED DO YOU BLAME ME?

HOW SHOULD A PERSON REACT?
WHEN FACED WITH THE FABULOUS FACT
A MARVEL LIKE YOU MIGHT CONSENT TO APPEAR
BUT NOT EVERY DAY OF THE WEEK
AND CERTAINLY NOT EVERY WEEK OF THE YEAR
  FLORA.
YOU'RE VERY PECULIAR
(*IN THE NICEST WAY POSSIBLE*)
I MEAN YOU'RE UNUSUAL
THAT IS TO SAY STRANGE
YOU'RE A HORSE OF ANOTHER COLOR
(*IN THE NICEST WAY POSSIBLE*)
IT'S REFRESHING TO MEET SOMEONE ODD
FOR A CHANGE

THOUGH I GRANT YOU AN APPLE
MAY NOT SEEM LIKE A LOT
IT'S A BEAUTIFUL APPLE
AND I HAVE TO ACKNOWLEDGE
IT'S NOT EVERY DAY OF THE WEEK
AND NOT EVERY WEEK OF THE YEAR
THAT SOMEONE WHOSE CHARMS
COULD BE SOMEWHAT GREATER
MEETS SOMEONE WHO SAYS TO HER
"HAVE AN APPLE—SEE YOU LATER"

HOW CAN I HELP BUT FEEL GOOD
YOU FIND ME ATTRACTIVE, KNOCK WOOD!
I MUST MAKE THE MOST OF THE MOMENT
   THAT'S HERE
ON ACCOUNT OF IT'S NOT EVERY DAY OF THE WEEK
AND HONESTLY NOT EVERY WEEK OF THE MONTH
AND CERTAINLY NOT EVERY MONTH OF THE YEAR!
   HARRY. I b-bet you pick-up a l-lot of strays. Cats. D-dogs.
   FLORA. Not a cat. Not a dog. They're not allowed. Just people.
(*dance*)
   FLORA/HARRY.
HOW CAN TWO PEOPLE REACT
WHEN FACED WITH THE FABULOUS FACT
THEY MUST MAKE THE MOST OF THE MOMENT
   THAT'S HERE
   HARRY.
ON ACCOUNT OF IT'S NOT EVERY DAY OF THE WEEK
   FLORA.
AND HONESTLY NOT EVERY WEEK OF THE MONTH
   FLORA/HARRY.
AND CERTAINLY NOT EVERY MONTH OF THE YEAR!

SCENE FIVE

The Park

[MUSIC #5a *MR JOB IN D (TRIO)*]

   ELSA/WILLY/MAGGIE. (*During the scene change*)
KEEP YOUR BLIND AMBITION
GO ON MAKE YOUR MARK
MISTER JUST GIVE ME A JOB

KEEP YOUR FANCY PENTHOUSE
HIGH ABOVE THE PARK
MISTER JUST GIVE ME A JOB
   WILLY. Three days later.
   ELSA/WILLY/MAGGIE. MISTER JUST GIVE ME A JOB

(*Harry sits on a park bench waiting for Flora. Behind him is a*

billboard advertisement for Lincoln Continental. Elegant people are draped around the car. It is cold and Harry pulls up his muffler.
Flora rushes on.)

FLORA. Sorry I'm so late.

HARRY. Any luck?

FLORA. Another waiting room. Catalogue work at Macy's. Ladies' underthings. Awful.

HARRY. Yeah? Well? (*They both sit on a bench.*)

FLORA. No go. At least thirty artists there to draw one set of drawers. I hope you're hungry. I brought lunch. (*She pulls a scarf filled with sandwiches from her bag.*)

HARRY. Where d-did you get all this!?

FLORA. Cheese sandwiches. Cheese sticks. Cheese puffs. They were having a cooking demonstration in housewares. Cooking with cheese. Luncheon is served. (*Tasting one.*) M-m-m. These are divine. Simply divine. So cheesy.

HARRY. You know, F-Flora, you shouldn't go to those interviews anymore. I'm n-not. They're too — what — d-degrading.

FLORA. Harry — how can you say that?

HARRY. Because I know that Garret and Mellick's has no intention of h-hiring mutts like us.

FLORA. Mutts?

HARRY. Yeah. And d-don't think they'd ever let you d-do your kind of artwork. It would never be accepted.

FLORA. Why?

HARRY. Because you're a nobody — yeah — s-starting at the bottom. And this system never gives the worker a fair shake.

FLORA. What system?

HARRY. The uh-uh-uh (*he points to the billboard.*) The Capitalistic system! Flora, last week I saw a crowd of fifty men and women fighting over a barrel of g-garbage outside the backdoor of a restaurant. American citizens fighting for food. It c-could have been us! It c-could have been cheese! Flora — there's s-something I just gotta tell you.

FLORA. You hate cheese! (*She gathers up the cheese.*)

HARRY. No. I'm a Communist.

FLORA. Huh!?

HARRY. And I took the liberty of bringing you an application to j-join the party. (*He gets out an application.*)

[MUSIC #6 *SIGN HERE*]

FLORA. Oh.
HARRY. Look at it this way, Flora . . .

ARE YOU IN FAVOR OF DEMOCRACY?
YOU MUST BE IN FAVOR OF DEMOCRACY
WELL, SINCE YOU'RE IN FAVOR OF DEMOCRACY
HERE, SIGN. SIGN HERE.

HOW DO YOU FEEL ABOUT THE RIGHTS OF MAN?
ARE YOU A SUPPORTER OF THE RIGHTS OF MAN?
WELL, IF YOU'RE IN FAVOR OF THE RIGHTS OF MAN
HERE, SIGN. SIGN HERE

FLORA.
I see it.

THE RIGHTS OF MAN
DEMOCRACY
THEN IT'S CLEAR! IT'S
  CLEAR!
YOU'RE A COMMUNIST!
  SIGN HERE

Gee Harry—I don't know
—I never thought—

DO YOU BELIEVE IN
  EVERLASTING PEACE? Yes!
YOU GOT TO BELIEVE
  IN EVERLASTING
  PEACE Of course I believe in
AND IF YOU BELIEVE   everlasting peace.
  IN EVERLASTING
  PEACE
HERE, SIGN. SIGN HERE

HOW ABOUT MILK AND
  COOKIES FOR THE KIDS Oh!
YOU WANNA HAVE
  MILK AND COOKIES Oh, yes!
  FOR THE KIDS?
WELL IF YOU WANT

MILK AND COOKIES
FOR THE KIDS
HERE, SIGN. SIGN HERE

FREE MILK FOR KIDS?
A LASTING PEACE?
THE RIGHTS OF MAN?
DEMOCRACY?
THEN IT'S CLEAR! IT'S
  CLEAR!
YOU'RE A COMMUNIST!
  SIGN HERE
THE WIND OF CHANGE
  IS BLOWING
THE TIDE IS ROLLING IN
AND WE'VE A RICHER,
  RIPER, FRESHER, FINER
WORLD TO WIN!

ARE YOU IN FAVOR OF
  SECURITY?
WHO ISN'T IN FAVOR
  OF SECURITY?
WELL, SINCE YOU'RE IN
  FAVOR OF SECURITY
HERE, SIGN. SIGN HERE

WOULD YOU MAKE
  CANNON FODDER OF
  OUR YOUTH?
YOU COULDN'T MAKE
  CANNON FODDER OF
  OUR YOUTH
WHO'D WANT TO MAKE
  CANNON FODDER OF
  OUR YOUTH?
HERE SIGN. SIGN HERE

PROTECT OUR YOUTH?
SECURITY?
FREE MILK FOR KIDS?

FLORA:
Oh!
Sure!

Harry!
What tide?
Harry!

HARRY!

Yes.

No one.

Cannon fodder?

Of our youth?

No one.

A LASTING PEACE?
THE RIGHTS OF MAN?
DEMOCRACY?
THEN IT'S CLEAR! IT'S
  CLEAR!
YOU'RE A COMMUNIST!
  SIGN HERE!

FLORA:
Harry, I don't think I
understand . . .

THE WIND OF CHANGE
  IS BLOWING
THE TIDE IS ROLLING IN
AND WE'VE A RICHER,
  RIPER, FRESHER, FINER
WORLD TO WIN

WHAT DO YOU THINK
  OF JOBS FOR
  EVERYONE?   I want a job for everyone.
OF COURSE YOU
  WOULD LIKE A JOB
  FOR EVERYONE
WELL IF YOU WOULD
  LIKE A JOB FOR
  EVERYONE
HERE, SIGN. SIGN HERE

HOW DO YOU FEEL
  ABOUT THE FILTHY
  RICH?   I HATE the filthy rich!
I KNOW HOW YOU
  FEEL ABOUT THE
  FILTHY RICH
AND IF THAT'S HOW
  YOU FEEL ABOUT
  THE FILTHY RICH
HERE, SIGN. SIGN HERE

NO FILTHY RICH?   I don't think it's so simple.

NO UNEMPLOYED? You've got to think about
PROTECT OUR YOUTH? the other answers.
SECURITY?
FREE MILK FOR KIDS?
A LASTING PEACE?
THE RIGHTS OF MAN?
DEMOCRACY?
THEN IT'S CLEAR! IT'S
  CLEAR!
YOU'RE A COMMUNIST!
  SIGN HERE

FLORA. Aw, Harry, listen. Just because I believe in all those things does that make me a Communist? After all, you don't think that everyone who believes those things is a member of the party now, Harry, do you? I mean—do you?

HARRY.
AND WE'VE A RICHER,
  RIPER, FRESHER,
  FINER WORLD TO WIN

FLORA:

HOW WOULD YOU LIKE
  TO DO AWAY WITH
  SLUMS? Oh!
OF COURSE YOU
  WOULD LIKE TO DO
  AWAY WITH SLUMS! I hate slums!
WELL IF YOU WOULD
  LIKE TO DO AWAY
  WITH SLUMS!
HERE, SIGN. SIGN HERE

WOULDN'T YOU WANT
  TO SAVE AMERICA? America!
OF COURSE YOU
  WOULD WANT TO
  SAVE AMERICA! I love America!
WELL, IF YOU WANT
  TO SAVE AMERICA
HERE, SIGN. SIGN HERE

AMERICA America!
AWAY WITH SLUMS Away with slums!

NO FILTHY RICH   No filthy rich!
NO UNEMPLOYED   No unemployed!
PROTECT OUR YOUTH?
SECURITY?
FREE MILK FOR KIDS
A LASTING PEACE?
THE RIGHTS OF MAN?
DEMOCRACY?
THEN IT'S CLEAR! IT'S CLEAR!
FIND THAT DOTTED LINE . . .
HERE . . . (*He kisses her. She signs.*)
SIGN!

[MUSIC #6a *WINDS OF CHANGE*]

SCENE SIX

The Studio
(*Elsa is working on the dress she showed us earlier. It is pinned to
    a dressmaker's dummy. The dress is not completely
    unattractive — however it is definitely of Elsa's own design.
Flora enters — a little stunned.*)

FLORA. (*Talking to herself.*) I am a Communist. (*She tries it
another way.*) Hello, I am a Communist. (*She extends her hand to
an imaginary person and shakes it.*) Yes, I am a Communist.
How do you do?

ELSA. (*Looking up.*) Oh Flora — Willy's been looking for you.
Where have you been?

FLORA. With Harry. (*She takes off her coat.*)

ELSA. What did you do?

FLORA. We talked. Ate a few cheese sandwiches. I joined the
Communist Party.

ELSA. What?!

FLORA. Oh really Elsa — (*she sits with her*) — everyone's a
Communist. Eleanor Roosevelt. Mahatma Gandhi. Chaing-Kai
Shek.

ELSA. Dollars to doughnuts, you're gonna get an earful about
free love.

FLORA. No. Oh no. Harry's serious.

ELSA. Oh no — I'M serious. (*Mr. Weiss enters.*)

MR. WEISS. Hello Flora.

FLORA. Mr. Weiss. I am a Communist.

MR. WEISS. That's nice. (*He turns to walk away. Flora is surprised. Then he turns around and begins in earnest.*) It was that Harry.

FLORA. Mr. Weiss.

MR. WEISS. I knew it. He tricked you, didn't he. Sure. While you weren't looking. So now it begins. He's going to start demanding this and that and that and this and pretty soon, we're going to be getting our little Flora out of trouble because of something crazy!

FLORA. Mr. Weiss, how do you know so much?

MR. WEISS. Because I'm older than all of you put together.

WILLY. (*Entering.*) Flora! Flora, where have you been?

FLORA. Willy, I'm a Com —

WILLY. Garret and Mellick's has been calling.

FLORA. What?

WILLY. A Mister Stanley — he called twice. You were supposed to be there an hour ago.

FLORA. (*She takes the note from Willy's hand as if she doesn't believe him. Then she turns to Elsa.*) Give me that dress. Who says I have to look like a mutt. You men turn around. (*Flora begins to rip off her dress.*)

ELSA. No — no — it's not really finished.

FLORA. And give me your shoes. (*Willy is standing there with his mouth open.*) Willy — I mean it. (*Willy turns.*)

ELSA. You can't walk in these.

FLORA. I'll learn. (*Elsa helps Flora change.*) Mr. Stanley called me! It's gotta be because of the sketches. He's going to offer me a job.

WILLY. (*He spins around.*) A job! (*Flora is in her slip and motions him to turn back around.*)

FLORA. He thinks he's going to get my work cheap. They all do when you start out. But I'm starting at $20 a week.

ELSA. $15 isn't bad.

FLORA. Okay. $15. No less.

KENNY. (*Kenny and Maggie enter.*) Hello everyone.

MAGGIE. Hi!

ELSA. Kenny, turn around. (*He does.*)

KENNY. What is this — a stick up?

ELSA. Flora got a job.

FLORA. A job interview—please.

MAGGIE. Oh! That's wonderful.

KENNY. Congratulations.

FLORA. Thanks! (*She reaches down to get her shoes. She stops halfway.*) Um—Elsa—what's wrong with this dress?

ELSA. (*Who is just finishing fastening the back of the dress.*) You can't bend over in this dress. You can't sit either.

FLORA. (*Determined.*) So I'll stand. (*She stands back up.*) Just tell me it looks good.

ELSA. Well of course it does. Now when are you coming back.

FLORA. Oh, El—can I get it to you tomorrow? (*Maggie helps Flora get into the shoes.*)

ELSA. Why?

FLORA. Because I have a meeting I'm supposed to go to tonight.

MR. WEISS. Here it comes.

WILLY. What meeting?

FLORA. A Communist Party meeting.

KENNY/MAGGIE/WILLY. WHAT?! (*They all turn around.*)

MR. WEISS. Flora—please—listen to me. You and Communism—it's like you and this dress. It's not a good fit.

FLORA. (*Not interested.*) Just tell me how I look. (*She tries to walk and nearly falls over.*) No don't. I don't want to know. (*She adjusts her way of walking and sashays across the studio to get her coat.*)

MR. WEISS. Well, you'll see. With the Communists, Stalin will sneeze and they'll all catch cold.

FLORA. (*As she exits.*) Just wish me luck.

ARTISTS. Good luck.

FLORA. (*Nearly hopping out of the studio.*) Good bye. Good bye! Good bye!

ELSA. Just be back by eight with my shoes!

MAGGIE. A Communist? Flora?

KENNY. Flora?

WILLY. Flora—the red menace! [MUSIC 6b *"MR JOB"* (*into Stanley Scene*)] (*He plays a lick on his clarinet as Kenny dances around Maggie like a Cossack.*)

ALL. Hey!

[MUSIC #6B *MR. JOB*]

(*As the new scene is being set, they sing:*)

I DON'T NEED TUITION
FOR ANY FANCY SCHOOL
MISTER JUST GIVE ME A JOB

FOLD THE GREEN UMBRELLA
BESIDE MY SWIMMING POOL
MISTER JUST GIVE ME A JOB

MISTER JUST GIVE HER A JOB

SCENE SEVEN

Mr. Stanley's Office
(*Mr. Stanley is seated at his desk.*)

SECRETARY. (*Entering.*) Mr. Stanley . . . Miss Meszar-ROS.

FLORA. (*She hobbles in behind the secretary. She corrects the secretary's pronunciation of her name.*) Mes-ZAR-ros.

MR. STANLEY. You're late. Please sit down. (*He motions to a chair near his desk.*)

FLORA. (*Trying to be sophisticated.*) One day, they say, we're going to be able to take dirigibles from one office building to the next and avoid all the —

MR. STANLEY. Yes. Please sit down. (*Flora hops over to the chair as Mr. Stanley looks at her samples.*) Now — are you working anywhere else.

FLORA. Countless offers. (*She tries to sit in the chair but can't. The more she tries to find a good angle to sit, the more ridiculous she looks.*) I have plans to go to Europe to study — study with the masters. You know the masters. They have so much to offer . . . don't they? Such a help to my career. (*She gives up and stands.*)

MR. STANLEY. I'd like to offer you a job.

FLORA. A job?!

MR. STANLEY. A job.

FLORA. (*The thought stuns her. Without thinking, she drops back into the chair. Her dress rips.*)

SECRETARY. (*At that moment, the secretary enters with a box of merchandise. She smiles too sweetly and places the box on Mr. Stanley's desk.*) Here's the merchandise you requested.

MR. STANLEY. Your artwork is fresh. It's good. Very good. Of course, you're going to have to modify it to the Garret and Mellick way of doing things.

FLORA. Of course.

MR. STANLEY. (*The secretary stands behind him. She picks a piece of lint off his suit.*) The campaign is based on the daughter of Mr. Garret. She is my fiance. (*The secretary stops and then, very coldly, walks directly out of the office. Mr. Stanley clears his throat and continues.*) The campaign is all about elegance.

FLORA. Oh, I do elegance very well.

MR. STANLEY. Good. (*He takes the dress out of the box. The beading catches the light.*) This is the dress for the first ad.

FLORA. Yow-sa!

MR. STANLEY. Now—I'll expect it on Monday at 9am. One thing you must understand . . .

[MUSIC #6c *MR. STANLEY'S VERSE*]

MR. STANLEY.
WHEN I SAY NINE O'CLOCK, THEN I MEAN NINE
  O'CLOCK
I DON'T MEAN NINE-O'FIVE OR TEN OR NINE-FIFTEEN
WHEN I SAY NINE O'CLOCK IT'S NINE O'CLOCK I MEAN

WHEN I SAY UP A THIRD, THEN I MEAN UP A THIRD
DON'T WANT TO KNOW WHAT OTHER METHODS
  YOU PREFERRED
IF I SAY UP A THIRD THEN PUT IT UP A THIRD

WHEN I SAY CHINESE RED THEN I MEAN CHINESE
  RED
I DON'T MEAN ORANGE, CORAL, RUST OR
  TANGERINE
YOU'LL FIND I ALWAYS SAY EXACTLY WHAT I MEAN
  SECRETARY. (*Offstage.*) Mr. Stanley—
  MR. STANLEY. Coming. For example . . .
  MR. STANLEY.
WHEN I SAY SOMETHING'S GOOD, I MEAN IT'S
  REALLY GOOD
SO WHEN I SAY IT'S BAD DON'T CRY AND MAKE
  A SCENE
BECAUSE I ONLY SAY EXACTLY WHAT I MEAN

SECRETARY. (*Offstage.*) Mr. Stanley —
MR. STANLEY. I'll be right there . . .
BE ACCURATE, DEPENDABLE, BEGINNING
  MONDAY AT NINE
AND WE'LL GET ALONG JUST FINE, MISS
  MAH-ZAROS, FINE
FLORA. (*Correcting his accent.*) Mes-ZAR-os.
MR. STANLEY.
MISS MESZAROS, FINE
SECRETARY. (*Offstage.*) Mr. Stanley!
MR. STANLEY. I'm coming. (*To Flora*) Oh — there is just one
more thing — your salary.
FLORA. Oh — that.
MR. STANLEY. $30 a week.
FLORA. $30 a week. (*Then it hits her.*)
MR. STANLEY. Is there anything the matter?
FLORA. (*She shakes her head.*) No!
MR. STANLEY. Good. Then welcome to Garret and Mellick's.
(*He leaves. She is all alone.*)

[MUSIC #7 *A QUIET THING*]

SONG: QUIET THING

FLORA.
WHADDYA CALL A JOB WITH GARRET AND
  MELLICK'S?
WHADDYA CALL A FASHION ILLUSTRATOR?
WHADDYA CALL ASSISTING MR. STANLEY? ME!
WHADDYA CALL . . . THIRTY DOLLARS A WEEK!
THIRTY! THIRTY! THIRTY! THIRTY!

I WANNA RUN . . . NO I DON'T
I WANNA SCREAM . . . NO I DON'T
I WANNA . . . I WANNA SIT DOWN
I DON'T HEAR ANYTHING
YOU'RE SUPPOSED TO HEAR BELLS, DRUMS,
  TRUMPETS
I DON'T HEAR ANYTHING
DO YOU HEAR ANYTHING? NO?
WELL, WHADDYA KNOW?

WHEN IT ALL COMES TRUE
JUST THE WAY YOU PLANNED
IT'S FUNNY BUT THE BELLS DON'T RING
IT'S A QUIET THING

WHEN YOU HOLD THE WORLD
IN YOUR TREMBLING HAND
YOU'D THINK YOU'D HEAR A CHOIR SING
IT'S A QUIET THING

THERE ARE NO EXPLODING FIREWORKS
WHERE'S THE ROARING OF THE CROWDS?
MAYBE IT'S THE STRANGE NEW ATMOSPHERE
WAY UP HERE AMONG THE CLOUDS

BUT I DON'T HEAR THE DRUMS
I DON'T HEAR THE BAND
THE SOUNDS I'M TOLD SUCH MOMENTS BRING
HAPPINESS COMES IN ON TIP-TOE
WELL, WHADDYA KNOW
IT'S A QUIET THING
A VERY QUIET THING

WHADDYA CALL A JOB WITH GARRET AND
   MELLICK'S?
WHADDYA CALL A FASHION ILLUSTRATOR?
WHADDYA CALL . . . THIRTY DOLLARS A WEEK!
THIRTY!

SCENE EIGHT

Communist Party Meeting

[MUSIC #7A *COMMUNIST VAMP*]

(*The scene begins as the members of the Party set up for the
    meeting. They talk to one another and are excited about the
    meeting.*
*A banner is hung which reads "Communism Is Twentieth Cen-
    tury Americanism."*)

GALKA. (*Pounding gavel.*) As chairman of the cell, I call this meeting to order. Comrade Patrick?

PATRICK. I've collected thirty-nine signatures which leads me to believe that within the month we'll have a good start on the union at Florsheim's. (*Everyone applauds. Galka pounds the gavel.*)

GALKA. And Comrade Esther?

ESTHER. (*She jumps up, clutching a stack of flyers.*) I've distributed 376 flyers — 375 of them to very friendly people getting off the Hudson River Day Line. (*Everyone applauds.*) Well, I would have done more — but oh! Number 376 . . . (*For a moment, she is enraptured in thought. She sighs . . . and then realizes everyone is watching. She sits.*) I'll have a better report next week. (*Everyone applauds.*)

GALKA. I'm sure you will. And now! The highlight of everyone's week! A report from Comrade Charlotte! (*Everyone applauds again.*)

[MUSIC #8 *THE FLAME*]

CHARLOTTE. Me? I did nothing. (*Everyone laughs. This isn't possible.*)

GALKA. You? Nothing? That will be the day.

CHARLOTTE. I did nothing . . . much.

CHARLOTTE.
ON MONDAY I PUT PICKETS ON TWENTY-SEVEN LINES
I ALSO STARTED RIOTS AT B. ALTMANS' SAKS AND KLEINS
I BROKE THREE WOOLWORTH WINDOWS, DESTROYED AN AUTOMAT
YOU'D THINK I'D BE ENTITLED TO A BREATHER AFTER THAT

(*The crowd rumbles. They agree. She looks up at them and they all stop.*)

BUT THEN I FELT THE FLAME
I FELT IT BURN INSIDE ME
LIKE A GLOWING TORCH TO LIGHT MY WAY
ALTHOUGH MY SHOULDERS DROOPED
AND I WAS PLENTY POOPED

I HEARD A LITTLE VOICE WITHIN ME SAY

YOU MUST DO MORE
YOU MUST DO MUCH MORE
YOU MUST GO ON
FOREVER PLAYING YOUR PART
YOU MUST DO MORE
YOU MUST DO MUCH MORE
UNTIL YOU'VE LIT THE FLAME
IN EVERY SINGLE HEART!

(*Everyone applauds. She cuts them off.*)

ON TUESDAY IN THE SUBWAY, I THREW A
   ROTTEN EGG
I CALLED A MAN A FASCIST AND I BIT HIS
   DAUGHTER'S LEG
I SPAT UPON A LANDLORD, I KICKED A TRAFFIC COP
AND LATER ON, IN NIGHT COURT, WHEN THE
   JUDGE SAID "CHARLOTTE STOP!"

(*The crowd rumbles.*)

   PATRICK. You didn't stop, did you? (*Charlotte looks at him. Again, everyone is quiet.*)
   CHARLOTTE.
AGAIN I FELT THE FLAME
I FELT IT BURN INSIDE ME
LIKE A GLOWING TORCH TO LIGHT MY WAY
THOUGH I'D ALREADY DONE
THE WORK OF TWENTY-ONE
I HEARD A LITTLE VOICE WITHIN ME SAY . . .

YOU MUST DO MORE
YOU MUST DO MUCH MORE
YOU MUST GO ON
FOREVER PLAYING YOUR PART
YOU MUST DO MORE
YOU MUST DO MUCH MORE
UNTIL YOU'VE LIT THE FLAME

IN EVERY SINGLE HEART!
  COMMUNISTS.
WE MUST DO MORE
WE MUST DO MUCH MORE
WE MUST GO ON, FOREVER PLAYING OUR PART
WE MUST DO MORE
WE MUST DO MUCH MORE
UNTIL WE'VE LIT THE FLAME
IN EVERY SINGLE HEART!

(Again, they all applaud. Again, Charlotte cuts them off.)

  CHARLOTTE.
JUST YESTERDAY ON WALL STREET, I MADE A
  LITTLE FUSS
SHORT-CIRCUITED A DUSENBERG AND WRECKED
  A CROSSTOWN BUS
THE STATEN ISLAND FERRY WAS WHERE I LATER
  SCORED
YOU'LL NEVER GUESS WHAT HAPPENED WHEN
  THEY THREW ME OVERBOARD.
  HARRY.
(He jumps up and
  impassionately sings.)
I k-k-know! I know. I JUST
  know!
I B-B-BET YOU F-FELT   CHARLOTTE.
  THE FLAME   Harry, sit down.
YOU F-F-FELT IT BURN
  INSIDE YOU   Harry, this is my story.
LIKE A G-GLOWING
  TORCH TO LIGHT
  YOUR WAY
YOUR MOUTH WAS
  F-FILLED WITH FOAM
BUT AS YOU SWAM
  BACK HOME
YOU HEARD A L-LITTLE
  VOICE WITHIN YOU
  SAY . . .

ALL.
WE MUST DO MORE
WE MUST DO MUCH MORE
WE MUST GO ON,
FOREVER PLAYING OUR PART
WE MUST DO MORE
WE MUST DO MUCH MORE
UNTIL WE'VE LIT THE FLAME
IN EVERY SINGLE HEART!

(*Dance to . . .*)

ALL.

UNTIL WE'VE LIT THE FLAME IN EVERY SINGLE
  HEART!

(*Dance to . . .*)

TODAY, TONIGHT, WE LIGHT THE FLAME!

(*The Communists applaud and gather around Charlotte. Flora
    rushes in with her coat on. She carries her bag and the box of
    merchandise from Garret and Mellick's.
Harry runs over to greet her. He is followed by Galka.*)

FLORA. Harry!
HARRY. Flora! Where have you been?
GALKA. So! The new member you were speaking of—
Comrade Harry—you do the introductions.
HARRY. Everyone—this is Flora Meszaros. She r-runs an art-
ists' cooperative—
FLORA. And I just got a job at Garret and Mellick's!
HARRY. You did?!
GALKA. Congratulations! (*Everyone comes over to congratu-
late her.*)
CHARLOTTE. Comrades! (*Everyone stops for a moment.*) It is
not a union shop.
GALKA. Maybe we could change that.
DARLA. How?

GALKA. Well, now that we have a comrade in the store — think of what we can do.

PATRICK. What do you suggest?

GALKA. Tell me, Flora — you think Garret and Mellick's is swell — don't you? (*He offers Flora a seat.*)

FLORA. Oh yes! (*The Communists gather around Flora.*)

GALKA. You'd like to make it the best place to work.

FLORA. Sure!

GALKA. A union place.

FLORA. Of course.

GALKA. Then all you have to do is just talk to a few people and collect a list of names of those interested in forming a union. They'd be protected by a union.

HARRY. Flora — YOU'D be p-protected by a union.

FLORA. It's important to you?

HARRY. It's important to you.

FLORA. Then I'll do it! (*Everyone applauds.*)

HARRY. (*Very proudly.*) She will, too!

FLORA. Once I set my mind to something it's smooth sailing.

HARRY. That's right, I know.

GALKA. And so at the next meeting, you'll bring in a list?

FLORA. Absolutely. (*Even more applause.*)

GALKA. Good.

CHARLOTTE. Oh Comrades, please. One lone little girl collecting names. What is this . . . the scouts?

FLORA. (*Fearlessly.*) No I can do it — really!

CHARLOTTE. (*Incredulous.*) YOU can start a union?

FLORA. I can try.

HARRY. Sh-she can try.

CHARLOTTE. (*She's had enough.*) If you are going to go after Garret and Mellick's you must act. Remember . . . broad strokes!

ALL. (*Repeating. A little ragged. A little tired.*) Broad strokes.

GALKA. (*Appeasing Charlotte.*) Then what do you suggest?

CHARLOTTE. (*She thinks for a moment.*) A rally. In front of Garret and Mellick's. (*Everyone likes this idea.*)

FLORA. No! No!

CHARLOTTE. Yes! Yes!

FLORA. Not a rally — not yet anyhow. I just started.

CHARLOTTE. (*Ignoring her.*) We'll set up tables. Serve coffee.

Get people to gather round.

FLORA. You gotta work from the inside!

CHARLOTTE. Esther — you can pass out your flyers! (*Everyone applauds enthusiastically.*)

FLORA. Wait a minute.

CHARLOTTE. (*Going for the kill.*) And Harry. YOU can speak.

HARRY. (*Stunned.*) Me? (*The group is stunned as well.*)

CHARLOTTE. Absolutely. (*She looks at the group and then they all applaud supportively.*) And *I'll* get employees to sign up. Perfect strangers.

HARRY.   Uh-you-uh-uh-you . . . you . . . want   m-me to . . . speak?

CHARLOTTE. Not to worry. As a favor to the party, I will work with you personally. Yes. Now. What do we say? (*Everyone applauds.*)

FLORA. (*Determined not to be written off.*) I say I can still try! I mean, you nipped me in the bud!

GALKA. (*Breaking the tension.*) Now now now — let's do both!

HARRY. That's a good idea. (*Everyone applauds.*)

GALKA. Say — February 16. It will be a great day for the party! (*Everyone agrees.*) Good. Then any further business? No? Then meeting adjourned. Thank you everybody!

ALL. (*Everyone gathers their things, folds up chairs and marches out.*)

PREPRISE: THE FLAME

WE MUST DO MORE
WE MUST DO MUCH MORE
WE MUST GO ON
FOREVER PLAYING OUR PART
WE MUST DO MORE
WE MUST DO MUCH MORE
UNTIL WE'VE LIT THE FLAME
IN EVERY SINGLE HEART!

HARRY. F-Flora — I'm so proud of you — I r-really am! (*Flora finally begins to take off her coat.*) I mean you j-just jumped right in there. You stuck to your guns. You've really g-got the spirit of the common man — (*She has taken off her coat. She wears the spectacular gown she is supposed to draw.*) Oh my god!

FLORA. What? Oh. This? It's for my job! (*She walks and dips across the room.*) It's what all the workers have to wear.

HARRY. Flora! It's-uh-um-you-

FLORA. Harry — please. I'm . . . kidding. My dress ripped and I put on this . . . shmatte. I'm supposed to draw it. Do you like it?

HARRY. (*He does. Very much.*) Well . . .

CHARLOTTE. (*Entering.*) Well, well, well, well. If it isn't Marie of Rumania. The new hope for the Communist Party.

HARRY. (*Horrified for Flora. he rushes over to her and puts her coat over her.*) Oh! The uh-uh-she-uh . . . she ripped. I mean — uh — she's kidding.

FLORA. (*Not helping.*) I'm a kidder.

HARRY. It's a — a — a —

FLORA. (*Whispering*) A shmatte.

HARRY. A shmatte. Sure.

CHARLOTTE. Yes. I can see that. Comrade Harry, I'd like to know when we can begin working on your speech.

HARRY. Oh! The speech. When would you like to?

CHARLOTTE. Immediately.

HARRY. Oh thank you — but — I c-can't. Flora and I have plans. We're going to celebrate. (*To Flora.*) I got a job today too.

FLORA. You did?!

HARRY. A new mural p-project at the post office at 110th.

FLORA. That's wonderful! (*She rushes to Harry.*)

CHARLOTTE. That's marvelous! (*She crosses between them and grabs Harry.*) An artist. How — extraordin-AIRE. Think of all you can do for the party. The posters. The banners. The portraits. Harry — I'd love to pose for you.

HARRY. Well — l-let's take things s-s-slowly.

CHARLOTTE. Yes. That's just the way I like to take things. Slowly. (*She smiles and exits.*) Good night.

HARRY. Flora! A job! Me!

FLORA. I'm so proud!

HARRY. And it's only the b-b-beg-beginning.

FLORA. The beginning. Yes.

HARRY. And now that you're a comrade — well — j-j-just think of what's a-a-a-ah-ahead.

FLORA. Ahead. Yes. That reminds me. (*She rushes to her bag.*) I brought you something.

HARRY. Gee — what is it?

FLORA. (*She gives him a small bag.*) Marbles.

HARRY. Oh. Th-anks.

FLORA. I read in the newspaper that if you practice with marbles in your mouth you can cure a stammer. (*Harry isn't sure if he's hurt. Flora, sensing this, tries to build his spirits.*) Like Demosthenes. He was a Greek. He was a famous Greek. He was a famous speaker.

HARRY. (*Touched.*) I'll t-try it.

FLORA. Good. (*Determined.*) Now Harry. About that celebrating. I want you to take me dancing. What do you say?

HARRY. Oh — well — jeeze — Dancing? I don't dance.

FLORA. Sure you do. You just spin around like this! (*She spins.*) Come on. Try it. It's just like walking. (*She begins to lead him. Harry doesn't dance. He tries the best he can.*) Well, you'll get it. (*She spins away, holding the hem of her gown.*) And then my gown flutters behind me — like in a movie. And then we go for the lift.

HARRY. Th-th-th-the — (*Flora runs toward him and leaps through the air.*) The LIFT! (*He spins around a few times, catching his balance.*)

FLORA. And then the music swells . . . swells . . . it's just swell.

HARRY. And then what?

FLORA. At midnight . . . (*they are about to kiss.*) . . . I leave you a glass slipper. (*She jumps out of his arms, shooting into the air.*) Oh my god!

HARRY. What!

FLORA. I've got to get out of here. (*She gathers up her things.*)

HARRY. So no glass slipper — what is it?

FLORA. These shoes — they're Elsa's. She's stuck at the studio. (*Flora runs off. Harry is just left standing in the middle of the room. Flora returns. She kisses him squarely on the mouth. She smiles and then runs off.*)

HARRY. (*He watches her go. Then he picks up the bag of marbles and absent-mindedly begins popping the marbles into his mouth, one by one.*)

[MUSIC #8b: *FLAME WITH MARBLES*]

HARRY.
AND THEN I FELT THE FLAME
I FELT IT BURN INSIDE ME
(He becomes unintelligible.)

LIKE A GLOWING TORCH TO LIGHT MY . . .

(*His mouth nearly full, he almost chokes on a marble. He spits out the marbles into his hand and triumphantly sings . . .*)

WAY!

(*As the lights fade, Harry begins jumping for joy in a crazy, jubilant jig. He is in love.*)

SCENE NINE

The Studio
(*Kenny and Maggie have been rehearsing.*)

KENNY. Five, six. Five, six, seven, eight. One and two, three and four, five and six, seven and eight and one and two, three and four, five and six, seven and eight. (*Stopping.*) No — wait a minute Maggie — it's more like ba-ba-ba-dum. (*He does the step.*)

MAGGIE. (*Trying the step.*) Ba-ba-dum?

KENNY. You've got to get that extra ba-ba-ba-dum. That's what makes it work.

MAGGIE. (*She tries again.*) Ba-ba-ba-dum.

KENNY. Close. Ba-ba-ba-behind.

MAGGIE. Ba-ba-ba-behind.

KENNY. That's right. Ba-ba-ba-behind. Ba-ba-ba-behind.

MAGGIE. (*She breaks away for a moment.*) You know, I still can't believe Flora's a Communist.

KENNY. (*He is determined to rehearse.*) Where did that come from?

MAGGIE. Ba-ba-ba-behind — you sound like Harry.

KENNY. F-F-Five, six, seven, eight. (*They continue dancing.*) Come on, concentrate.

MAGGIE. I can't imagine she's a very good Communist.

KENNY. Why not?

MAGGIE. Well, you know Flora — (*Again Maggie stops.*) She might say to you "Yes! Absolutely!" But she'll go off and do things exactly as she pleases.

KENNY. That's true. Come on. Five, six, seven, eight. (*And they are off again.*) It's going to take more than the Communist Party to change Flora.

MAGGIE. There's more than that involved here.

KENNY. What.

MAGGIE. Love, Kenny.

KENNY. Love?

MAGGIE. It's just around the corner. And it can drive people to do the craziest things.

KENNY. What do you mean?

MAGGIE. What do you mean "what do I mean." (*Kenny spins her around and then she dips.*) Take a look at us.

(*Flora enters. She wears a sensational full-length fur coat.*)

MAGGIE. (*Absolutely shocked.*) Flora! What are you wearing!

KENNY. Where did you get that?

FLORA. Hello kids. (*As grand as the coat she wears.*) How are you? May I be the first to shake the hands of two potential celebrities.

KENNY. Who?

FLORA. You.

MAGGIE. What?

FLORA. Well, well, well. This morning, I went to Garret and Mellick's—you know them. Swell boys. Swell. And I picked up this coat they had on hold for me.

KENNY. You bought it?!

FLORA. (*As herself.*) No, no—I'm supposed to draw it. (*Resuming.*) And I went over to the Rainbow Room, I met with the talent booker, told him I was an agent and said . . . "DAH-ling—tell me. How good do you think a dance team would have to be for me to afford a coat—like this—at five per cent of their earnings." And he says "Pretty damn good." And I say, "DAH-ling, you DON'T know!"

KENNY. So?!

MAGGIE. So!?

FLORA. (*As herself.*) So you got an audition!

KENNY. You're kidding!

FLORA. February 16—you'll see if I'm kidding.

MAGGIE. I don't believe it!

FLORA. Work from the inside—that's what they say. It doesn't pay to wait in waiting rooms. (*They begin jumping and screaming, hugging one another. Suddenly, Kenny stops.*)

KENNY. February 16th. That's in four days! We gotta get to work. (*They begin to run out and then stop and scream.*)

KENNY/MAGGIE. The Rainbow Room! (*They exit.*)

HARRY. (*He rushes on, very concerned.*) Are you alright?

FLORA. Harry! (*She laughs.*) It was just Kenny and Maggie and . . .

HARRY. (*He smiles.*) Hi.

FLORA. Hi.

HARRY. Are you r-ready to go? (*He hands her an apple.*)

FLORA. Let me see — am I ready to go. Go where?

HARRY. P-Passing out pamphlets?

FLORA. (*She forgot.*) Oh.

HARRY. Before the meeting? On the pier? Did you forget?

FLORA. No — not exactly. (*She puts the apple into a small cupboard on a shelf. When she opens the cupboard doors, we see a half dozen or so other apples.*)

HARRY. Well?

FLORA. I have to finish my artwork — you know — my first assignment and all. (*She gets her artwork out of her bag, sits and then begins to put a few finishing touches onto it.*)

HARRY. You s-said you had to have that in this morning.

FLORA. Well — I g-got a little sidetracked.

HARRY. And what about the n-names.

FLORA. What about the names.

HARRY. From Garret and Mellick's.

FLORA. They're fine. Just fine. In fact, I was going to do more at the store right now.

HARRY. Good. And what did you think of tonight's reading assignment? (*He sits next to her.*)

FLORA. Oh . . . I had a little trouble with it. (*She hasn't read it.*)

HARRY. (*He realizes this and begins playing with her.*) Free enterprise. Free society. Free will. Trouble?

FLORA. Oh yes. All those . . . "free's." Free wheeling. Free for all. Free . . . parking.

HARRY. That's right. All those "free's." And what about . . . free love? (*This was not in the reading.*)

FLORA. Free love?

HARRY. Certainly . . . it's very important to the party.

FLORA. Free love?

HARRY. Maybe we could talk about it after tonight's meeting.

FLORA. Talk about it?

HARRY. M-maybe at my apartment.

FLORA. Oh . . . well—Harry. I don't know. I mean—that would be impossible. You see—it's just that I've—

HARRY. Aw, Flora—there's nothing to it.

FLORA. To it?

HARRY. Nah.

FLORA. All the same, maybe I should just plan on staying in tonight. Really bone up on that assignment. I always like to read everything three or four times. I mean, I'm still a vir—valedictorian.

HARRY. Oh, Flora—there's n-no need to go to all that. We could s-skip the reading assignment. We c-could just f-f-f-foxtrot.

FLORA. (*She hasn't really heard him.*) Foxtrot!

HARRY. Dancing!

[MUSIC #9 *NOT EVERY DAY-REPRISE*]

FLORA. (*Relieved.*) Oh!

HARRY. Sure!

FLORA. I love to dance.

HARRY. I'm ready for another lesson.

FLORA. (*She takes Harry's hands and begins doing a simple box step.*) Kenny taught me this. You have to make a box.

HARRY. A box?

FLORA. Watch my feet. That's it. (*Gradually, Harry gets into the rhythm of the step. He is elated.*)

HARRY. We're dancing?

FLORA. Yeah!

HARRY. We're dancing! I saw this in a movie. (*Holding Flora's hands, Harry guides Flora under his arms, around and the two end up in a knot.*)

FLORA. What movie? "The Hunchback of Notre Dame?" (*They unscramble, not letting go of each other's hands, and spin around to their original position. They abruptly come face to face.*)

HARRY.

HOW SHOULD TWO PEOPLE REACT

FLORA.

HOW SHOULD TWO PEOPLE REACT

HARRY.

WHEN FACED WITH THE FABULOUS FACT

HARRY/FLORA.
THEY MUST MAKE THE MOST OF THE MOMENT
THAT'S HERE

(*They kiss very tenderly.*)

HARRY/FLORA.
AND CERTAINLY NOT EVERY MONTH OF THE YEAR

(*And then they begin dancing slowly, Flora's head on Harry's shoulder. The lights fade.*)

[MUSIC #9a *NOT EVERY DAY TAG*]

SCENE TEN

An elevator at Garret and Mellick's

(*Flora steps onto an elevator which is defined by a square of light on the floor.*
The elevator operator sits on a crate. A man stands near the back of the elevator reading a newspaper.)

OPERATOR. (*A bell rings.*) Going up?
FLORA. Twelve please. Administrative offices.
OPERATOR. (*The elevator begins with a jolt.*) Hey, you're new here.
FLORA. Just started. You been here long?
OPERATOR. Enslaved here's more like it.
FLORA. Well, whaddya think about a union?
OPERATOR. (*Wincing.*) I wouldn't use words like that around here. People might think you're a red. (*The elevator jolts as it stops at a floor. The operator opens the door. A bell rings.*) Watch your step.
MR. STANLEY. Twelve please. (*Flora hides behind the man's newspaper.*)
OPERATOR. Yes sir. (*The elevator jolts.*)
MR. STANLEY. Miss Meszaros. (*The newspaper is lowered.*

Flora smiles.) I expected you three hours ago. Let me see your artwork.

FLORA. You mean here?

MR. STANLEY. Would you rather go to Gimbel's? (*The bell rings. The elevator stops. Three customers get on, all carrying large packages.*)

CUSTOMER. Eight please.

FLORA. (*She struggles with her bag, taking things out and handing them to people in the elevator.*) Excuse me, could you hold this please. I think you'll like it. It's so much more high fashion. (*Handing Mr. Stanley the artwork.*) Don't you think I captured the romance of the gown?

CUSTOMER. Oh it's lovely.

FLORA. Thank you.

MR. STANLEY. (*Looking at it.*) But I want details! Where are the details? The stitching, the buttons, the trim, the accessories, the background, the setting—this just won't do!

FLORA. But that's my style.

MR. STANLEY. And I told you to modify it. You didn't listen.

OPERATOR. (*The bell rings.*) Eight. (*The customers rush off.*)

MR. STANLEY. Women will only buy dresses they can understand. How to put on and then take off again. Do you think the ordinary woman is going to understand this?

FLORA. No. I mean yes!

OPERATOR. (*The bell rings.*) Twelve.

MR. STANLEY. (*Getting off the elevator.*) Miss Meszaros. I'll give you one more opportunity. I'll expect it at 9am on Wednesday morning. Good day.

(*Mr. Stanley's Secretary walks past. The two bump into one another.*)

MR. STANLEY. Oh—hello, Miss Williams.

SECRETARY. Mr. Stanley. (*He leaves. She gets onto the elevator.*)

SECRETARY. Miss Mes-zar-ROS.

FLORA. Miss Will-YUMS.

SECRETARY. (*To elevator operator.*) Seven please. Ladies foundation garments.

FLORA. Such a grand word for a girdle. Foundations. (*Then.*) Sorta sounds like you've got bricks in your panties.

[MUSIC #10 *NOW IT'S FEBRUARY*]

*(Willy, who has been playing the elevator operator, steps forward
    and sings as the scene changes.)*

WILLY.
BECAUSE IT'S FEBRUARY
THAT'S A CERTAIN SIGN
SOMEONE WILL BE ASKING
"BE MY VALENTINE"

SCENE ELEVEN

The Studio
*(Elsa is posing for Flora. She wears the gown from Garret and
    Mellick's.)*
ELSA. Oh Flora — you've got five more minutes. God! Am I
hungry.
FLORA. I'm almost done — and stop wiggling.
ELSA. I've got to fit Maggie into her audition dress.
FLORA. Okay, okay.
ELSA. So what are you and Harry doing for Valentine's Day?
FLORA. We're taking a buggy ride through Central Park. Of
course, he doesn't know it yet. It's a surprise.
ELSA. That's nice. Hey, is that a box of chocolates I see?
FLORA. Don't even think about it.
ELSA. I'm not going to eat it. I'm just going to look at it. Sniff it.
(She picks up the box of candy and looks at the card.)
FLORA. It's a Valentine's gift for Harry.
ELSA. "My dearest Valentine . . ." Can I read this?
FLORA. Read what?
ELSA. ". . . just a little marzipan from your loving Tarzan-
man. . . " Jesus. Who wrote this?
FLORA. Give me that. *(Taking note.)* It's from Mr. Stanley.
ELSA. To you?
FLORA. No! It was on his desk —
ELSA. You stole it!
FLORA. Oh Elsa, he was just giving it to his secretary —
ELSA. Miss Polka Dots?
FLORA. Yes!
ELSA. Well, I hope he's good looking — he can't rhyme worth
beans.

FLORA. And to think he's engaged to the boss' daughter.

ELSA. Do you think (*she raises an eyebrow*) Miss Polka Dots and him?

FLORA. Oh, Elsa!

ELSA. On the desk?

FLORA. On my sketches?!

ELSA. I wouldn't be surprised!

FLORA. NO! (*The two laugh and scream like school girls. Charlotte and Harry enter. They wear matching red scarves.*) Charlotte!

CHARLOTTE. Flora!

HARRY. Hi—uh—she—w-wants to s-see my m-mural sketches. Charlotte, I'd l-like you to meet Elsa. And of course you know F-Flora.

CHARLOTTE. We go way back. (*Reminding him.*) Sketches?

HARRY. Oh! It's—it's—over there. (*She exits.*)

FLORA. (*Pulling lightly on Harry's scarf.*) Where'd you get this?

HARRY. This? Charlotte knit it for me. Keep my throat warm at the rally.

FLORA. Charlotte? (*She yanks the scarf, nearly choking Harry.*)

ELSA. Flora—

FLORA. (*To Harry*) It's lovely. (*And then she flings the scarf back over his shoulder.*)

CHARLOTTE. (*Re-entering.*) Harry—your work is . . . remarkable! (*She grabs Harry by the shoulders.*)

HARRY. You think it will l-look g-good in the post office?

CHARLOTTE. It makes me want to run out and lick stamps. (*Flora is angry all over again. Elsa, sensing a scene, grabs Flora by the arm.*)

ELSA. Flora—get me out of the dress.

FLORA. Now?

ELSA. You heard me. (*She drags Flora out of the room.*)

CHARLOTTE. You know, Harry—you should really be working with the artists at the Daily Worker. They are all sharing a studio near the office.

HARRY. I'm doing just fine here.

CHARLOTTE. But how do you keep from being distracted?

HARRY. Well, it's not a problem . . .

CHARLOTTE. HOW can you possibly work on your speech?

HARRY. Uh—well—actually I w-was going to do that at my apartment.

CHARLOTTE. Tonight?

HARRY. Yes.

CHARLOTTE. Good. Then I'll just come on over and help.
HARRY. Oh no no no no no — you don't have to do th-that.
CHARLOTTE. No no no no — it's my treat.
HARRY. Honestly.
CHARLOTTE. Honestly. Just give me a couple of hours to take care of a few things and I'll see you later.
HARRY. Uh-I-um-ah-ah-I
CHARLOTTE. Harry, you don't have to walk me to the subway.
FLORA. (*Re-entering.*) That's right, Harry — she's a big girl.
CHARLOTTE. That's right Harry — I'm a big girl. (*She exits.*)
FLORA. I don't trust that woman.
HARRY. She's very committed.
FLORA. She ought to BE committed.
HARRY. To the cause.
FLORA. Cause?! She's a piranha — and she's after you.
HARRY. Aw — F-Flora — (*changing the subject.*) You're s-still planning to pose tomorrow for m-me with the others?
FLORA. Yes. With a sickle in one hand and Charlotte's head in the other — and DON'T change the subject.
HARRY. F-Flora — I have to go.
FLORA. Go! Harry, you just got here! I thought we were celebrating Valentine's Day.
HARRY. I still have to p-p-practice my speech.
FLORA. Harry —
HARRY. I was painting banners all day at the party office with Charlotte and I d-didn't — get a chance to — I'm . . . I'm sorry. (*He gives her a small daisy.*) Happy Valentine's Day. (*He leaves.*)
FLORA. (*She looks at the flower and then calls out after him.*) That's right, Harry. You don't want to disappoint Comrade Charlotte.

[MUSIC #11 *DEAR LOVE*]

FLORA. Comrade Charlotte. Well, Harry. It's time you knew the absolute truth. I cannot STAND Comrade Charlotte. Charlotte. Charlotte. CHARLOTTE! CHARLOTTE! CHARLOTTE! CHARLOTTE! Do you know what "Charlotte" rhymes with, Harry? HARLOT! Talk about your masses. THERE is a mass for you. What were you and Comrade Charlotte just talking about, Harry? Rights? People's rights? How everybody's got rights? You've got rights. She's got rights. We've all got rights. Well, Harry. I've got news for you. This is Valentine's Day. I've got rights, too!

FLORA.
DEAR LOVE
WILL YOU SAY BE MY VALENTINE?
DEAR LOVE
ARE YOU MAYBE MY VALENTINE?
THIS DAY COULD FOREVER BE WRITTEN ON THIS
   HEART OF MINE
IF THIS DAY I AM YOUR VALENTINE

I know. I'll go over to his apartment. It's February 14th. It's Valentine's Day. It's also HIGH time! (*She grabs her coat and the box of candy.*) You want to F-F-F-oxtrot Harry? I'll show you how to Foxtrot.

DO YOU KNOW HOW YOU FEEL ON THE VERY
   FIRST DAY OF MAY, HARRY
WHEN YOU ARE GETTING READY TO MARCH IN
   YOUR PARADE
YOU KNOW, EXCITED AND HAPPY AND WARM
   ALL OVER, HARRY
WELL, THE WAY THAT YOU FEEL ON THE FIRST
   DAY OF MAY
IS THE WAY YOU COULD FEEL ON THIS
   FOURTEENTH DAY OF FEBRUARY
I MEAN HAPPY, VERY

(*She exits. Street lamps come on and we are now outside.*)

CHORUS.
DEAR LOVE
WILL YOU SAY BE MY VALENTINE?
DEAR LOVE
ARE YOU MAYBE MY VALENTINE?
THESE EYES COULD BE LIT WITH A NEW AND
   TRULY DAZZLING SHINE
IF YOU'D SAY I AM YOUR VALENTINE
   FLORA.
IF THAT ROOM UP THERE WERE MINE
I'D BOLT THE DOOR AND ONLY ALLOW MY
   HARRY IN

FURTHERMORE, I'D WEAR A SIGN, A SIGN THAT SAYS
"THIS PROPERTY IS PROPERTY OF COMRADE H.
  TOUKARIAN"
CHORUS.
DEAR LOVE, DEAR LOVE
DEAR LOVE, DEAR LOVE
THIS DAY COULD FOREVER BE WRITTEN ON THIS
  HEART OF MINE
IF THIS DAY I AM YOUR VALENTINE
FLORA.
WELL THE WAY THAT YOU FEEL ON THE FIRST
  DAY OF MAY
IS THE WAY I COULD FEEL ON THIS FOURTEENTH
  DAY OF FEBRUARY
I MEAN HAPPY, VERY
MR. STANLEY. (*He passes.*) Miss Meszaros!
FLORA. (*Surprised. She hides the candy box behind her back.*)
Mr. Stanley (*Then calling out to him.*) Happy Valentine's Day.
CHORUS. (*Offstage.*)
DEAR LOVE
FLORA.
DEAR LOVE
CHORUS.
DEAR LOVE
DEAR LOVE

(*Flora pulls up her collar as it lightly begins to snow.*)

END OF ACT ONE

INTERMISSION

[MUSIC #11a *Entr'acte*]

ACT TWO

SCENE ONE
(*As the lights come up, Kenny and Maggie are in position, ready to perform the routine they have been working on for their Rainbow Room audition. Elsa and Mr. Weiss watch. Willy is ready to accompany them on the clarinet.*)

ELSA. (*As if she were a radio announcer.*) Live! From the Hotel Sedgewick! The incomparable dance team! Kenny and Maggie! (*Everyone applauds.*) Okay, now do it exactly like you're going to do it at the audition.
MAGGIE. Okay.
MR. WEISS. Don't mind us.
MAGGIE. We won't.
ELSA. We're not even here.
KENNY. Alright already!
WILLY. Okay. Here goes nothing.

[MUSIC #12 *KEEPIN' IT HOT*]

KENNY.
THOUGH IT MAY SOUND MORE THAN DRASTIC
I CAN'T WAX ENTHUSIASTIC
OVER A GIRL WHO DOESN'T SEE THINGS MY WAY
SO MY PET IN THAT CONNECTION
I'VE A CERTAIN PREDILECTION
I HAD BETTER MENTION
KINDLY PAY ATTENTION
I'M KEEPIN' IT HOT
I'M LETTIN' IT SIZZLE
IF YOU WANT TO DANCE ALONG WITH ME, I'M
KEEPIN' IT HOT

IF HOT YOU ARE NOT
WE'RE CERTAIN TO FIZZLE
YOU CAN ONLY GET IN STRONG WITH ME, BY
KEEPIN' IT HOT

DOWN WITH WALTZES
AND THAT OLD-FASHIONED THREE-QUARTER TIME
I'M NOT HAPPY
UNLESS THE RIFF IS SWINGY AND SPIFFY

I LIKE YOU A LOT
YOU COULD BE MY PARTNER
BUT IF YOU'RE DISINCLINED TO TAG ALONG
OR TO TRUCK ON DOWN AND SHAG ALONG
PLEASE DON'T WASTE MY TIME, I'M
KEEPIN' IT HOT

MAGGIE.
I HAVE HEARD EACH WORD YOU'VE TOLD ME
BUT YOU'RE PREMATURE TO SCOLD ME
'SPECIALLY SINCE, I FEEL THE WAY THAT YOU DO
YOU WILL MEET WITH NO DEFIANCE
THIS IS NOT A MISALLIANCE
YOU WON'T HAVE TO QUIT ME
THAT SAME BUG HAS BIT ME

I'M KEEPIN' IT HOT
I'M LETTIN' IT SIZZLE
TELL THAT CLARINET TO BLARE FOR ME, I'M
KEEPIN' IT HOT

IF HOT YOU ARE NOT
I'M CERTAIN TO FIZZLE
ASK THE BAND TO SHOW THEY CARE FOR ME, BY
KEEPIN' IT HOT
BOTH.
DOWN WITH WALTZES
AND THAT OLD-FASHIONED THREE-QUARTER TIME
I'M NOT HAPPY
UNLESS THE RIFF IS SWINGY AND SPIFFY

I LIKE YOU A LOT
YOU COULD BE MY PARTNER
MAGGIE.
PARDON ME, BUT MAY I TAG ALONG
KENNY.
YES INDEED, WE'LL TRUCK AND SHAG ALONG

AS WE MAKE IT CLEAR, WE'RE
  BOTH.
KEEPIN' IT HOT

[MUSIC #12a *HOT DANCE*]

(*Dance to . . .*)

  BOTH.
I LIKE YOU A LOT
YOU COULD BE MY PARTNER
PARDON ME BUT MAY I CHUG ALONG
LINDY HOP OR BUNNY HUG ALONG
AS WE MAKE IT CLEAR, WE'RE
KEEPIN' IT . . .
HOT!

(*Willy, Elsa and Mr. Weiss applaud.*)

[MUSIC #12b *"HOT" PLAYOFF*]

(*As the scene changes, Willy plays a clarinet solo. When the scene is set . . .*)

WILLY. Later that evening—in Harry's apartment.

SCENE TWO

HARRY'S APARTMENT
(*Harry is on his bed, speaking dramatically and loudly with marbles in his mouth. He pretends he is speaking before a crowd. His room is barren. Perhaps a single light bulb hangs from the ceiling. Charlotte knocks at the door (a free-standing unit which has been rolled on during the scene change.)*)

CHARLOTTE. Harry? (*More knocking.*) Harry? (*She is very determined.*) HARRY! (*She bursts into the room. Harry jumps into the air.*) Good god Harry! I thought you were being murdered!
HARRY. (*Spitting the marbles into his hand.*) Marbles. I was practicing m-my speech.

CHARLOTTE. Of course. (*She smiles. Then slams the door behind her.*) May I come in?

HARRY. Oh-uh-uh-um-you-uh (*He nervously pulls at the blankets on the bed. Charlotte takes off her coat and waits for Harry to take it from her. She looks around.*)

CHARLOTTE. (*She is not impressed.*) So.

HARRY. So.

CHARLOTTE. Are you ready?

HARRY. Ready?

CHARLOTTE. To work!

HARRY. Oh-I-uh-yes-well

CHARLOTTE. Can we sit?

HARRY. Oh-um-uh-uh-uh

CHARLOTTE. Can I sit?

HARRY. Would you like to sit?

CHARLOTTE. A cot! (*She sits. Harry nervously tries to retain some level of protocol.*) How Spartan. Just like the Cossacks on the front. Tell me. Do you ever play . . . "Soldier and Spy?"

HARRY. N-no.

CHARLOTTE. Would you like to learn?

HARRY. Would you like to hear my speech?

CHARLOTTE. It's very simple. I am the spy and I have something important to tell you.

HARRY. I've been working very hard.

CHARLOTTE. I'm sure you have. Now. Can you guess what my secret is?

HARRY. Secret?

CHARLOTTE. (*She pulls him onto the bed.*) We are in a bombed out farmhouse. The moon shines. The enemy is all around. In the distance, you can hear the "Hoo Hoo" of an owl. And suddenly, I turn to you and I say . . . "Comrade, do you know that Comrade Charlotte is being recruited to run for party secretary!" And you say . . . and you say . . .

HARRY. (*He is very surprised and trying to keep the encounter on the up and up, he takes her hand and vigorously shakes it.*) Uh-um-I-I

CHARLOTTE. Close. And then I say ". . . Comrade, do you know WHOM she is recommending to take her place?" And you say . . .

HARRY. Uh-uh-uh—

CHARLOTTE. Close again. You!

HARRY. (*He jumps up.*) ME?! You're recommending m-me!?

CHARLOTTE. That's right. And now—soldier—a deal's a deal. It's your turn to tell me the news—(*she stands and takes off her blouse. She wears a lacey camisole.*) From the front.

[MUSIC #13 *EXPRESS YOURSELF*]

HARRY. News?
CHARLOTTE. Come sit.
HARRY. Where?
CHARLOTTE. Close. (*She pulls the scarf she knitted for him around his neck.*)
CHARLOTTE.
SITTING ALONE LIKE THIS
THINK OF THE SPARKS WE'D SET LOOSE
IF YOU WOULD ONLY LET LOOSE
EXPRESS YOURSELF!

IF YOU WOULD STEAL A KISS
NONE OF THE NEWS WOULD LEAK OUT
THIS IS THE TIME TO SPEAK OUT
EXPRESS YOURSELF!

IT'S THERAPEUTIC YOU WILL FIND
(IF YOU KNOW WHAT I MEAN)
WHEN ONE IS WILLING TO UNWIND
(IF YOU KNOW WHAT I MEAN)

I THINK IT'S SIMPLY BLISS
HERE IN YOUR SMALL DOMINION
TELL ME, WHAT'S YOUR OPINION?
EXPRESS YOURSELF

GET OFF OF THAT LOCAL TRAIN
IT'S SLOW AS CAN BE, AND
EXPRESS YOURSELF TO ME!

CHARLOTTE. Loose, Harry. Relax! Go all over limp. Now what have you got to say?
HARRY. Uh-I-well-wha

CHARLOTTE. Good! Settle back. Oops. Now talk baby. (*She blows in his ear.*)

HARRY. Ha! You b-blew in my ear!

CHARLOTTE.
I'M AT YOUR MERCY AS YOU SEE
(*IF YOU KNOW WHAT I MEAN*)
WHY NOT BE MERCILESS WITH ME
(*IF YOU KNOW WHAT I MEAN*)

YOURS IS THE KIND OF SMILE
I'M WILLING TO SUCCUMB TO
SO WOULDN'T YOU BE DUMB TO
REPRESS YOURSELF?

PULL INTO THAT PARKING PLACE
RIGHT HERE ON MY KNEE, AND
EXPRESS YOURSELF TO ME

CHARLOTTE. (*Harry crawls under the bed.*) Harry, where are you?! Are you playing soldier and spy? (*She pulls the blanket off the bed and flings it around herself like a cape and then crosses to the other end of the bed, blocking Harry's escape.*) I have an important secret to tell you. (*Face to face with Harry, she screams*). Ah ha! (*Harry begins backing up under the bed. Charlotte jumps on the bed, tip-toeing across the mattress.*) Soldiers crawling through the jungle. (*And then, when Harry emerges from under the bed, Charlotte jumps on his back.*) AMBUSH! (*She slides down his body and grabs onto his leg.*) I am your prisoner! Take me! (*Harry, trying to shag her, drags her across the room.*)

CHARLOTTE.
LOOSEN THE TIES THAT BIND
FAN EVERY FLAME INSIDE YOU
LET LENIN'S SPIRIT GUIDE YOU
UNDRESS YOURSELF

(*Charlotte jumps up and pulls on Harry's sweater. He falls onto the bed. Charlotte grabs the blanket and jumps onto the bed.*)

CHARLOTTE.
WHATEVER OCCURS TO YOU
FEEL PERFECTLY FREE, AND

EXPRESS YOURSELF TO ME
(*IF YOU KNOW WHAT I MEAN!*)

(*She holds the blanket over her head and at the end of the song, pulls it over Harry, taking him prisoner. Charlotte laughs at Harry's attempts to escape. There is a knock at the door. While still under the blanket, both of them sit up with a start.*)

CHARLOTTE. Who is it?

FLORA. (*Calling through the door.*) Harry?

HARRY. It's Flora! (*He tries to get out from under the blanket.*)

CHARLOTTE. Good god, Harry — she's out after curfew. (*She has Harry in her grip and won't let up.*)

HARRY. (*He pokes his head out from under the blanket.*) Coming! (*Charlotte pulls it back under.*)

CHARLOTTE. Tell her . . . you're tied up.

HARRY. (*Beginning to swing his arms.*) I've got to get the door.

FLORA. Harry, I brought you something.

HARRY. (*Calling to her.*) Just a minute. Charlotte — please!

CHARLOTTE. (*Enjoying this very much.*) Tell her your head is in the clouds.

FLORA. Is something the matter?

HARRY. No! Charlotte please. Let go of my — th-th — (*They continue to struggle under the blanket. Charlotte laughing. Harry pleading. And then, inadvertently, Harry punches Charlotte in the face. Charlotte is still for a moment and then slowly tips over — backwards — head first. The blanket becomes very still.*) Uh oh. (*Harry jumps out from under the blanket.*) Comrade? Oh please don't do this to me — p-please —

FLORA. Mr. Valentine. Mr. Valentino.

HARRY. Just a minute. (*He tips Charlotte over, flipping her legs over her head and then begins to push her under the bed.*)

FLORA. Knock knock.

HARRY. Who's there.

FLORA. Flora.

HARRY. Flora who?

FLORA. Flora minute there, I thought you weren't home.

HARRY. (*He puts the blanket on the bed.*) You're such a card. (*Nervously looking around the room making sure everything is in order.*) No — uh — it was j-just a question of — d-dirty laundry . . . (*He opens the door — very calm and collected.*) Why Flora! Wh-what a lovely surprise!

FLORA. You're surprised? (*Then.*) So am I. (*She is still not in the room.*) Happy Valentine's Day. (*She gives Harry the box of candy and waits for an invitation into the room. Harry slams the door.*) HARRY!

HARRY. Oh!

FLORA. Can I come in? (*He opens the door. She waltzes in. She gives him her hat.*) Tres Bo-he-me-AN! Just like I imagined it! (*She begins to slip off her coat. Harry puts it back on and gently guides her to the door.*)

HARRY. How about a c-cup of coffee?

FLORA. (*She spins back into the room.*) And no place to sit down. Except for this . . . bed.

HARRY. (*Putting her hat back on.*) Flora, I'll m-meet you in the automat. Just give me a few minutes.

FLORA. (*Taking off her coat and sitting on the bed.*) I don't want to go to the automat. Besides Harry—I brought you a special Valentine's gift.

HARRY. Oh you d-didn't have to do that.

FLORA. Can you guess what it is? (*She smiles.*) It's ME!

CHARLOTTE. (*She moans under the bed.*)

HARRY. (*Stamping his foot on the floor.*) Neighbors. The most d-disgusting noises!

FLORA. (*As Flora spins her fantasy, Charlotte's hand emerges from under the bed nearly grabbing Flora's foot. Harry crosses to the bed and sits next to Flora, batting Charlotte's hand away. Charlotte keeps groping Harry's leg.*) I've decided you're right. I mean, what am I so afraid of? They say that—you know—it's just like learning to drive a car. You just turn the key and step on the gas and before you know it—you're tearing lickety-split down love's highway. I read that in a book.

HARRY. (*Charlotte grabs Harry's thigh.*) Oh god! (*He pulls her hand away.*)

FLORA. Well, sort of. It was written by a clergyman. (*Charlotte grabs Flora's knee. Thinking it's Harry's hand, she shuts her eyes, thrilled beyond belief.*) Oh—Oh Harry . . . (*She takes Charlotte's hand and waits to be kissed. Nothing happens. Then she opens her eyes and sees both of Harry's hands in a position of prayer. Flora stops smiling. Then she looks down at the hand she is holding. The two are frozen for a moment and then both of them scream and jump off the bed.*)

HARRY. Comrade Ch-Charlotte! (*Charlotte crawls out from under the bed.*)

FLORA. WHAT! IS SHE DOING HERE?!

HARRY. We w-were just p-practicing.

FLORA. Practicing what?!

HARRY. My-my-my elocution.

FLORA. Elocution?

CHARLOTTE. Look it up. (*She is completely disheveled and still a little groggy. She heads for the door.*)

HARRY. Wait—C-Comrade—please. (*He rushes to get her coat and scarf.*) Before you go I just had two or three more ideas—I m-mean for the speech—and uh—(*He puts the coat over her and seems to be making matters worse.*) And what about that re-recommendation to the p-party.

CHARLOTTE. In the words of the immortal Lenin: "VPERED K POBEDE KOMUNIZMA. NICHTO NE ZABYTO I NIKTO NE ZABYTO." (*"Forward to the victory of Communism. Nothing is forgotten and no one is forgotten."*)

HARRY. What's that mean?

CHARLOTTE. Forget it.(*She exits.*)

HARRY. Flora—

FLORA. Don't bother saying anything.

HARRY. It's n-not what you think.

FLORA. Of course it isn't.

HARRY. You have to believe me.

FLORA. THEN WHY DID YOU HAVE THAT TROJAN HORSE UP HERE?!

HARRY. Now, F-Flora—

FLORA. (*She tries to get her things together and wrestles with her coat.*) And to think of it! I actually came over here—ready to go—ready to be—thinking I—thinking HEY! I got a Valentine! I'm finally going to show him just how much I care!

HARRY. She was here for the p-party.

FLORA. Some party!

HARRY. No—r-really—for my speech.

FLORA. Then Harry, since your speech is so important to you—it's good night, good bye, Happy Valentine's Day and have FUN tonight playing with your marbles! (*She whips the box of candy at him and storms out of the room, leaving the door open.*)

HARRY. (*Slowly, Harry sits on the bed. He is completely bewildered. Lost. He addresses the audience directly as he sings:*)

[MUSIC #14: *WHERE DID EVERYBODY GO?*]

HARRY.	FLORA.
WHERE DID	(*She is on the street, beneath*
EVERYBODY GO?	*a streetlamp.*)
YOU LOOK AT THOUGH	

YOU KNOW
SO WON'T YOU KINDLY   FLORA.
TELL ME   TELL ME

DON'T SIT THERE
LOOKING WISE

FLORA.
WHAT DO YOU
SUPPOSE I SAID

HARRY.
IT'S RIGHT BEFORE
YOUR EYES

FLORA.
BESIDE HIM ON THE BED

HARRY.
SO WON'T YOU PLEASE
EXPLAIN

WHY DID THEY TREAT   THAT MADE HIM
ME   TREAT ME

THIS WAY   THIS WAY

CHARLOTTE.
(*She, too, is on the street,
holding her ever-blackening
eye.*)

THIS WAY
THIS WAY BUSTER
LET THERE BE NO DOUBT

FLORA.
WHENEVER AN
ACCIDENT HAPPENS
IT HAPPENS TO HAPPEN
TO ME!

CHARLOTTE.
THIS WAY, HARRY

HARRY, THIS WAY OUT!

HARRY.
OUT OF MY MIND
I'LL GO OUT OF MY MIND
WHY?

FLORA.
OUT OF HIS MIND
HE'S GONE OUT OF HIS
MIND

CHARLOTTE.
DAMMIT, IF ONLY HE
  WEREN'T SO CUTE

FLORA.
YOU'VE GOT TO
  WONDER WHY

HARRY.
THIS WHOLE M-M-MESS
  IS A B-B-B-BEAUT

CHARLOTTE.
I THOUGHT HE WAS SO
  SHY

FLORA.
APPLES TURN OUT TO
  BE TREACHEROUS
  FRUIT

CHARLOTTE/HARRY/FLORA.
I NEED TO KNOW THE
  ANSWER

(*They all cross and come together in the middle of the stage
  and stand side by side.*)

HARRY.
COMRADE FLORA

FLORA.
COMRADE CHARLOTTE

CHARLOTTE.
COMRADE HARRY

(*They all cross their arms simultaneously, starting off with the "up yours" motion and then folding their arms across their chests.*)

ALL.
UP THE BOURGEOISIE
BUT WHY
UP ME?

(*They turn and exit. On the last note, Harry slams the door.*)

[MUSIC #14a *"MR. JOB" GOLF/PERFUME*]

(*During the scene change, Willy steps forward and sings.*)

WILLY.
I DON'T NEED YOUR GOLF CLUBS
I DON'T NEED YOUR LINKS
MISTER JUST GIVE ME A JOB

KEEP YOUR FANCY PERFUME
ME, I THINK IT STINKS
MISTER JUST GIVE ME A JOB
MISTER JUST GIVE ME A JOB

SCENE THREE

The Studio
(*Kenny, Maggie, Willy, Elsa and Mr. Weiss are all posed in an extremely revolutionary pose. Maggie holds a bundle of rags shaped like a baby. Kenny reaches for the sky. Willy holds his clarinet as if it were a gun. Elsa is underfoot. Mr. Weiss is not happy. A piece of drape is woven among all of them like a revolutionary flag.*
Everyone is tired. Harry sketches franticly.)

HARRY. M-Maggie, could you hold the b-baby a little higher? Remember, there's a promise of a g-good crop — you're dreaming of —
MAGGIE. A sequin gown.
HARRY. Full c-corn siloes and f-fat pigs.

ELSA. Isn't that nice.

HARRY. And Kenny—you're—

KENNY. Yes?

HARRY. You're—

ELSA. You're stepping on my chains. (*She pulls at some dress trim which has been wrapped around her wrists.*)

KENNY. Ooo—I'm sorry.

ELSA. You're forgiven.

HARRY. That's good.

WILLY. And to think we look like we're going to take over the world.

MR. WEISS. World nothing. We look like the post office is falling in. (*They resume the pose in earnest.*)

FLORA. (*Entering. Carrying a box of trim.*) Hello everyone.

ARTISTS. (*With revolutionary zeal.*) Hello Flora!

FLORA. (*Very chilly.*) Harry. (*Then.*) Elsa I have some trim for Maggie's dress. I found it in a bin behind the store.

ELSA. (*Breaking from the group.*) Just what we needed!

MAGGIE. (*Following Elsa.*) Kenny, hold the baby. (*She tosses the baby into the air, Kenny catches it.*)

ELSA. It's perfect.

MAGGIE. Around the bottom?

ELSA. No, around the top. Harry, you're going to have to excuse us. (*Maggie and Elsa exit.*)

(*Harry looks at the remnants of his tableaux. They all snap back into a new position—equally as dramatic.*)

WILLY. Protect the baby!

HARRY. (*Realizing it is pointless to go any further.*) We c-can stop now. Thanks.

KENNY. (*tossing the baby to Harry.*) Besides—I think it needs changing.

MR. WEISS. The revolution has ended. The troops retreat.

WILLY. (*Putting his clarinet into Mr. Weiss' back.*) March. (*To Kenny*) We take prisoner to automat. (*The three grab their coats and march out.*)

HARRY. Look, Flora—about l-last night and everything.

FLORA. Truce.

HARRY. No—I j-just wanted to say—

FLORA. You don't have to say anything.

HARRY. Really—I want to explain.

FLORA. No explanations.

HARRY. Flora —

FLORA. What's to explain. A woman under your bed? Perfectly natural. Everybody has one.

HARRY. Flora, please — it l-looked like s-something happened — but — I'm — I'm — I'm sorry.

FLORA. (*She is touched.*) Oh. (*But not willing to give in.*) Then on your knees.

HARRY. (*He gets on his knees.*) Flora Meszaros. I — Harry Toukarian —

FLORA. Who is sometimes a slouch.

HARRY. Who is sometimes a —

FLORA. Say it.

HARRY. A slouch.

FLORA. Thank you.

HARRY. And from the very very b-bottom of my heart — I want to say . . . Charlotte!

(*Charlotte enters.*)

FLORA. Of course.

CHARLOTTE. (*She wears a pair of sunglasses.*) Comrade Harry. I was up all last night — thinking about what I said — and I decided to make my recommendation to party leadership after all.

HARRY. Oh — thank you.

CHARLOTTE. Why let such a little thing get in the way of the party. I've also taken the liberty of writing your speech for you. (*She pulls out a piece of paper with the speech on it and gives it to Harry.*)

HARRY. (*A little disappointed.*) Oh.

CHARLOTTE. Which I think you should start working on right away. By yourself. I'll just watch. It begins . . . "Workers of the world unite." It's a beautiful beginning.

HARRY. Flora —

FLORA. No — go ahead. I don't want to stand in the way of the party. Besides, I'm going to the store right now to collect names. (*She gets ready to leave.*) And then at tomorrow's rally how surprised you'll be when you see all the names I've collected INSIDE the store — perfect strangers — and all the trouble you've gone to for nothing. Good bye, Harry. Charlotte. (*She leaves.*)

CHARLOTTE. (*Not pleased. She takes off her sunglasses, revealing her black eye.*) I question her principles.

HARRY. Principles?

CHARLOTTE. What else is the measure of the kind of Communist she is?

HARRY. Oh! She's principled.

CHARLOTTE. Yes—but for the sake of the party?

HARRY. (*Almost gloating.*) Oh yes. Just as soon as she turns in that artwork tomorrow she'll be out on the streets with us—side by side—at the rally.

CHARLOTTE. Side by side. (*The thought repulses her.*) That artwork. It's important she turns it in on time?

HARRY. Nothing could stop her.

CHARLOTTE. Oh. Well. (*Almost to herself as she exits.*) Then we'll see about that.

[MUSIC #14B *WINDS AND CHANT*]

(*As the scene changes, we hear the voices of strikers offstage.*)

WOMAN. Garret and Mellick!
ALL. Garret and Mellick!
WOMAN. Unfair!
ALL. Unfair!
WOMAN. Garret and Mellick!
ALL. Garret and Mellick!
WOMAN. Unfair!
ALL. Unfair!
WILLY. (*stepping onto the stage.*) The next day . . .
ALL. (*Gradually fading.*) Unfair, unfair, unfair . . .

SCENE FOUR

The Studio—the next day
(*Flora is hard at work. Mr. Weiss enters. She doesn't notice him.*)

FLORA. (*She is going over her list of names.*) Thirty. Thirty-one. Thirty-two. Thirty-three names. Including me.

MR. WEISS. (*Entering.*) Good morning Flora. (*He takes off his coat.*)

FLORA. (*She quickly shoves the names into a large blue Garret and Mellick envelope. She puts the envelope on her desk.*) Hello Mr. Weiss.

MR. WEISS. (*Coming over and taking a look at her artwork.*) Whose artwork is this?

FLORA. It's mine.

MR. WEISS. No it's not.

FLORA. For today it is. They don't like my style. So I had — to alter it a little.

MR. WEISS. You? Change your style? (*Looking at it.*) But your style is so — Paris. And this is so — Poughkeepsie.

FLORA. (*She doesn't want to talk about it. Kindly.*) I'm running a little late. (*She puts the artwork into a blue Garret and Mellick envelope as she crosses away from Mr. Weiss, leaving the envelope with the names on the desk.*)

MR. WEISS. Did Comrade Flora find time to sleep last night?

FLORA. Only a little.

MR. WEISS. If you slept "only a little" you should have slept less and used the time to finish. You must MAKE time. Isn't that what the party says?

FLORA. (*She laughs. And then dares to ask.*) Mr. Weiss — you were a Communist, weren't you. (*The two sit down beside one another.*)

MR. WEISS. Me? A Communist? (*Then.*) How could I not have been a Communist — with the world the shape it's in. We were looking for answers just like you. And they have answers. Answers to everything. But you know, Flora — you and I — we're alike. Sure. I say to you, "Your watch will be ready — maybe Thursday." And that's good enough for us. But "Maybe Thursday" wasn't good enough for them. It's Thursday or not at all. Thursday and you better be ready to fight. Thursday with fifty names. But I learned. Flora — there's more than one way to see red.

(*Willy rushes in — out of breath. He carries a large tux box.*)

WILLY. Hi! (*Calling to the other side of the studio.*) Hey — Kenny — I got the dinner jacket! (*He puts the tux box on the table, covering the envelope with the names. He takes out the dinner jacket.*)

ELSA. (*Entering with Maggie and Kenny.*) It's about time.

KENNY. Great!

ELSA. We've been waiting.

FLORA. (*Without thinking, she gives the envelope with the artwork in it to Willy as she takes the tux. She holds it up.*) Will you look at this?! (*Everyone is thrilled. In all the excitement, Willy puts the envelope with the artwork onto the top of the box.*)

WILLY. (*As Kenny puts on the coat.*) I would have been here earlier but my friend the trumpet player who owns this, was stuck all night at a Brenda Frazier party on Long Island. Said his car broke down. But . . . you know trumpet players.

ELSA. Perfect fit.

KENNY. Thanks Willy. You're the cat's pajamas.

MAGGIE. Thanks!

ELSA. Come on, Maggie—let's get you into that dress. (*Elsa takes the box—which contains the envelope with the artwork—and exits with Kenny and Maggie.*)

MR. WEISS. You did good, Willy.

WILLY. Some big doings going on down at Garret and Mellick's.

FLORA. Oh! The rally. Harry's going to be speaking.

WILLY. Rally! It's a picket-line. Cops. Banners. You name it.

FLORA. No. It's just a rally.

WILLY. I know a picket-line when I see one—and I wouldn't go down there if I were you.

FLORA. Yes but if I don't turn in my artwork, I'll be fired. (*Elsa re-enters.*)

MR. WEISS. "But Comrade! A picket line is a picket line."

FLORA. But I can't cross a picket line.

ELSA. Why not?

FLORA. Because I'd be kicked out of the party that's why not. (*Then.*) Unless someone else crosses the line for me. Then it doesn't matter. Does it. Willy, here. (*She gives him some money and the blue Garret and Mellick envelope which is on her desk.*) Take a cab. Garret and Mellick's. The twelfth floor. Mr. Stanley's office. Don't let anyone stop you. Get that artwork in on time.

WILLY. (*As he runs out the door.*) Yeah—sure. (*He exits.*) I got it. I got it.

MR. WEISS. Flora. You should have gone yourself. You've got your reasons. You don't have to do everything the party says.

ELSA. He's right, you know.

FLORA. But the party says—

MR. WEISS. Party! Party schmarty. You can't be everything to everybody!

FLORA. But—
ELSA. You can only be one person.
MR. WEISS. Now Flora, please. Listen to us.

[MUSIC #15 *YOU ARE YOU*]

MR. WEISS.
YOU ARE YOU
YOU ARE NOT SOMEONE ELSE
SOMEONE ELSE IS SOMEONE ELSE
YOU ARE YOU

FIX YOUR NOSE, BLACK YOUR TEETH
BUT THE PARTY UNDERNEATH STILL IS YOU
IT MAKES NO MATTER WHAT YOU DO
YOU ARE YOU

Right Elsa?
ELSA. That's right!

YOU ARE YOU
YOU ARE NOT MR. WEISS
MR. WEISS IS MR. WEISS
YOU ARE YOU

THEY CAN BLEAT, THEY CAN BRAY
BUT THEY CANNOT TAKE AWAY WHAT IS YOU
WHO CARES WHAT POSE YOU FALL INTO
MR. WEISS/ELSA.
YOU ARE YOU
FLORA. But the party says specifically—
ELSA.
LET THEM TELL YOU WHAT IS GOOD, WHAT IS NOT
MR. WEISS.
WHAT IS COLD, WHAT IS HOT
ELSA.
WHO TO LOVE, WHO TO HATE, WHO TO HIT
MR. WEISS.
WHEN TO BOW
BUT IT'S TIME THEY UNDERSTOOD
ELSA.
THEY CAN RAVE

MR. WEISS.
THEY CAN RANT
ELSA.
BUT THEY CAN'T GET A PURSE MADE OF SILK
FROM THE EAR OF A SOW
FLORA.
Thank you very much.
MR. WEISS.
That's correct.
ELSA.
Very true.
MR. WEISS.
Think it over.
ELSA.
WHO ARE YOU?
MR. WEISS.
WHO ARE YOU?
MR. WEISS/ELSA.
WHO ARE YOU?
FLORA.
I AM ME?
I AM NOT SOMEONE ELSE
SOMEONE ELSE IS SOMEONE ELSE
I AM ME

SNAP IT HERE, SNAP IT THERE
TAKE A PICTURE ANYWHERE
IT IS ME
FLORA.
NOT HIM, NOT YOU, NOT US, NOT WE
MERELY ME

I AM SICK OF ALL THE STRAIN AND THE WALKS
  IN THE RAIN
AND THE PAIN OF RETAINING THOSE DAMN
  REVOLUTIONARY RHYMES!
AND THE MOVIES THAT THEY SHOW WHERE
  THEY FORCE YOU TO GO
LIKE WHO ELSE DO YOU KNOW WHO HAS SEEN
  "POTEMKIN" THIRTY-SEVEN TIMES?!
MR. WEISS. What a task.
FLORA. Do not ask.

ELSA. Tsk. Tsk. Tsk.
MR. WEISS. Tsk. Tsk. Tsk.
MR. WEISS/ELSA. Tsk. Tsk. Tsk.
FLORA. I agree!
I AGREE!
I AM ME
I AM NOT MYRNA LOY
MYRNA LOY IS MYRNA LOY
I AM ME

THEY CAN BLEAT THEY CAN BRAY
BUT THEY CANNOT TAKE AWAY WHAT IS ME
ALL RIGHT SO NOT A LAMB
BUT I AM WHAT I AM
    ELSA/MR. WEISS.
I AM ME!
    FLORA.
I AM ME!
    ALL.
I AM NOT SOMEONE ELSE
SOMEONE ELSE IS SOMEONE ELSE
I AM ME

PAINT IT GREEN, PAINT IT RED
STICK A FEATHER IN ITS HEAD
IT IS ME
    FLORA/ELSA.
NOT HIM
    FLORA/MR. WEISS.
NOT HER
    ELSA/MR. WEISS.
NOT SHE
    ALL.
NOT THEM, NOT THEY, NOT WE
    FLORA.
IT MAY NOT BE A LOT
BUT WHAT ELSE HAVE I GOT
I AM ME!
    ELSA.
I AM ME!
    ALL.
I AM ME!
    KENNY. (*Offstage.*) May we have a drum roll please!

MR. WEISS. Yes sir! (*Kenny and Maggie enter. They are ready for their audition and look spectacular.*)

ELSA. Oh my goodness—am I in the right studio?

MAGGIE. I feel like I'm in the movies. Elsa—this dress is unbelievable!

ELSA. And worth every penny.

KENNY. Well, here goes nothing.

ELSA. Here goes something!

FLORA. You're not kidding.

MR. WEISS. Maggie—I got these out for you—they're from the shop. (*He gives her a pair of earrings.*)

MAGGIE. Mr. Weiss—I couldn't—

MR. WEISS. Don't say anything—go on take them—a star should glitter a little. (*Maggie gives Mr. Weiss a kiss.*)

KENNY. (*Handing Flora the envelope.*) Oh Flora—you left this on top of the box.

FLORA. Oh! The list of names! How could I have let them out of my sight?

KENNY. Names?

MAGGIE. No—it's artwork.

FLORA. No it's not. (*She takes the envelope and opens it.*) Oh my god. Oh my god! Oh my god! I sent Willy to the store with the list of names of people interested in joining the union. I've got to get down there. (*She grabs her coat.*) Maggie and Kenny—good luck! (*She exits.*)

MR. WEISS. Good luck she says. She could use a little luck herself.

[MUSIC #15a *"WINDS" INTO RALLY*]

SCENE FIVE

The Rally
(*Harry is standing on a soap box. He is very nervous and holds the speech Charlotte gave him. He tries several times to begin the speech.*)

HARRY. Wo-wo-workers of th the—(*He starts again.*) Workers of th-th-th-the—(*And again.*) Workers of the world—unite!

PASSER-BY #1. (*Offstage.*) Aw come on—get off the sidewalk!

HARRY. (*Again.*) W-w-w-workers of the world u-unite!

Passer-By #2. You're blocking traffic.
Harry. Y-Y-You have nothing to —
Passer-By #3. Come on buddy — give it a rest.
Harry. N-Nothing to l-lose —
Passer-By #4. Nothing to what?
Harry. Lose!
Passer-By #5. Yeah? Lose this! (*People laugh hysterically and continue to laugh through the first part of the song.*)
    Harry. (*He considers getting down for a moment. Then he crumples up the speech and throws it aside. He looks back out into the crowd.*)

[MUSIC #16 *THE JOKE*]

    Harry.
I DON'T BLAME YOU FOR LAUGHING
WHEN I SPEAK, I'M A JOKE
I KNOW
I DON'T BLAME YOU FOR LAUGHING
I'D LAUGH TOO
BUT WHILE YOU'RE LAUGHING . . .

(*He holds in his fist the bag of marbles which Flora gave him.*)

LISTEN . . .

THERE ARE PEOPLE OUT THERE
WITH NO SHOES ON THEIR FEET
WHO FIND SHELTER IN DOORWAYS
FROM THE SNOW AND THE SLEET
AND THEY SEARCH THROUGH THE GARBAGE
TO FIND SOMETHING TO EAT
AND THAT'S NO JOKE

THERE ARE PEOPLE OUT THERE
WHO MUST LIVE IN A TENT
AND THEIR EYES ARE ALL OLD
AND THEIR BODIES ARE BENT
AND THERE ISN'T A THING
THEY COULD GIVE UP FOR LENT
AND THAT'S NO JOKE

WELL, I SAY THAT'S LOUSY
WHILE VANDERBILTS DRINK CHAMPAGNE IN
  THEIR FANCY DIGS
YES, I THINK THAT'S ROTTEN
THAT SOME PEOPLE STILL LIVE HIGH ON THE HOG
WHILE SO MANY LIVE LIKE PIGS

BUT IF WE CAN UNITE
IF WE MAKE OURSELVES STRONG
IF WE'RE WILLING TO FIGHT
WE CAN RIGHT WHAT IS WRONG
OUR OPPRESSORS WILL KNOW
FROM THE WORDS OF OUR SONG
THAT THE JOKE IS ON THEM!
THE JOKE IS ON THEM!

(*Harry looks around. No one is listening. Slowly, he gets off the
    crate. Then, beginning with just one voice, people begin to
    enter and gather around.*)

WOMAN #1.
THERE ARE PEOPLE OUT THERE
  MAN #1/WOMAN #1.
WITH NO SHOES ON THEIR FEET
WHO FIND SHELTER IN DOORWAYS
FROM THE SNOW AND THE SLEET
  WOMAN #1, #2/MAN #1, #2.
AND THEY SEARCH THROUGH THE GARBAGE
TO FIND SOMETHING TO EAT
  ALL.
AND THAT'S NO JOKE
  HARRY.
WELL, I THINK THAT'S LOUSY
WHILE PLUTOCRATS SIT AROUND ON THEIR
  CUSHIONED BUTTS
YES, I THINK THAT'S ROTTEN
THAT SOME PEOPLE ACT LIKE PEDIGREE PETS
WHILE SO MANY FEEL LIKE MUTTS
  ALL.
BUT IF WE CAN UNITE
IF WE MAKE OURSELVES STRONG
IF WE'RE WILLING TO FIGHT

WE CAN RIGHT WHAT IS WRONG
OUR OPPRESSORS WILL KNOW
FROM THE WORDS OF OUR SONG
THAT THE JOKE IS ON THEM
THE JOKE IS ON THEM!

[MUSIC 16a *"JOKE" Playoff*]

(*The people shake Harry's hand and congratulate him. Then, several join the offstage picket line in front of Garret and Mellick's. We see the long shadows of the picketers against the back wall. Flora rushes on, hoping not to be noticed. Harry notices her and grabs her arm.*)

HARRY. (*He is thrilled.*) Did you hear me speak?!
FLORA. (*A little nervous. Distracted.*) Were you nervous?
HARRY. I could hardly open my m-mouth at first — but they listened!
FLORA. Of course.
HARRY. They cheered! They cheered M-ME!
FLORA. Some rally!
HARRY. Oh — well, Charlotte thought a picket line would look better for p-party leadership. (*He takes a picket sign.*)
FLORA. That Charlotte — always thinking.
HARRY. Get a picket sign from Esther. March with m-me. We'll see what scabs cross Flora.
FLORA. (*As if nothing were the matter.*) There's some business I have to take care of first.
HARRY. Where?
FLORA. In the store.
HARRY. Flora — this is a picket-line!
FLORA. (*More seriously.*) I think I turned in the list of names of people interested in the union by mistake.
HARRY. "You think?"
FLORA. Okay — so "I know."
HARRY. D-don't you see what you're doing?
FLORA. I'm saving a couple dozen people their jobs.
HARRY. You're c-crossing the picket line.
FLORA. One of them being my own.
HARRY. It doesn't work that way. That's the whole r-reason we have picket lines.
FLORA. Aw come on, Harry — this isn't a picket line. It's Charlotte's SPITE line. Face it.

HARRY. If you c-cross the picket line, Flora, you'll be sh-showing your disloyalty to the party. You'll be showing your disloyalty to m-me.

FLORA. It has nothing to do with disloyalty to you. I'm loyal. I'll STILL be loyal. I've got other people's JOBS on the line.

HAPPY. We're talking about p-principles.

FLORA. You're questioning my principles?

HARRY. Yes.

FLORA. Who the hell gave you the right to do that?

HARRY. Whether you see it or not, Flora, for the f-first time we have the chance to make a difference.

FLORA. Of course we do!

HARRY. And the only way we're going to get anywhere is if w-we accept the discipline of the party.

FLORA. Discipline has nothing to do with it! Ten years from now we'll be able to say we got someplace because we fought with our eyes open. NOT because we were disciplined.

HARRY. You're j-just afraid to make the sacrifice. Afraid to m-make the party the most important thing in your life.

FLORA. It is. To me! And that's my choice. But I'm not going to make that choice for people whose jobs I'm putting on the line. Harry—you can't be so black and white about this. The party does not have solutions to everything.

HARRY. Look—I have to g-go. You make your own decision. Either you are against us . . . or you are with us. But if you're against us—you're against me.

FLORA. So. That's what it comes down to. Cross this line and you've gone too far. Cross this line and the party will step in and say "You two can't be together because you don't approach everything in the same way."

HARRY. Yes.

FLORA. Well, Harry—if that's what you say—if that's what the party says—then I think the party stinks and I hate it because it makes you weak!

(*Flora considers for a moment what she has said and then crosses the picket line. Harry is left alone onstage, watching her go. He listens to the chanting of the picketers and then joins in with them.*)

WOMAN. (*Offstage*) Garret and Mellick!
ALL. Garret and Mellick!

WOMAN. Unfair!

ALL. Unfair!

WOMAN. Garret and Mellick!

ALL. Garret and Mellick!

WOMAN. Unfair!

ALL/HARRY. Unfair! Unfair! (*Gradually fading*) Unfair! Unfair!

(*We immediately segue to Mr. Stanley's office.*)

SCENE SIX

Mr. Stanley's Office

(*He is seated at his desk. Flora rushes on.*)

MR. STANLEY. (*Standing.*) Well, well, well. Miss Meszaros.

FLORA. Mr. Stanley —

MR. STANLEY. Please sit down. (*She does. He is extremely kind to her.*) I was just reading this article that I thought you might find interesting. An A&P in Cleveland just shut down its stores for several days and docked all the employees for lost time. And do you know why? Just to show them what they might expect if they joined a union. Isn't that interesting? Now, at Garret and Mellick's, how do you think we could make the same point? Close down the store? No. We'd have to find proof of a union. Like a list of names.

FLORA. I want to explain —

MR. STANLEY. And so, thanks to you, we'll be firing only those thirty-three people foolish enough to get involved.

FLORA. Mr. Stanley, I turned in that list by mistake. You can't fire those people.

MR. STANLEY. Oh? Union rules?

FLORA. You can't think that by firing anyone you're going to stop people from demanding what they need.

MR. STANLEY. (*Angered.*) I GIVE them what they need! A paycheck every week. The rest is just social work!

FLORA. Social work?

MR. STANLEY. Exactly.

SECRETARY. (*Entering.*) Here they are — all thirty-three of them. (*She gives him a stack of letters and exits.*)

FLORA. Social work?

MR. STANLEY. That's what I said.

FLORA. Is that why you have a social secretary?

MR. STANLEY. Excuse me?

FLORA. "My dearest Valentine—just a little marzipan from your loving Tarzan-man."

MR. STANLEY. What?

FLORA. "To the jungle beat we'll rumbah—later in my hut you'll succum-bah." Do you recognize it?

MR. STANLEY. Where'd you get that note?

FLORA. And to think you're planning to marry the boss' daughter.

MR. STANLEY. You give me that note.

FLORA. Not on your life. Not until you meet with your employees and listen to their demands.

MR. STANLEY. Oh that is impossible!

FLORA. (*Picking up the phone.*) Very well. Hello. Yes. Get me Mr. Garret's office please.

MR. STANLEY. You wouldn't dare.

FLORA. Mr. Stanley, you seem to forget. I have a very individual style.

MR. STANLEY. (*Slams his hand onto the receiver. Then he takes the phone, clicks the receiver a few times.*) Miss Williams, there's been a bit of a change. We won't be sending out those letters after all.

FLORA. Good.

MR. STANLEY. All except Miss Meszaros'. (*Putting his hand over the phone.*) That's the deal.

FLORA. Then . . . that's the deal.

MR. STANLEY. Miss Williams, I'm coming out to see you immediately. (*He hangs up the phone, signs one of the letters and gives it to Flora.*) Good bye Miss Meszaros.

FLORA. Good bye Mr. Stanley. (*He exits. Still sitting, she looks at the letter.*) "And your services are no longer required at Garret and Mellick's."

(*The strikers come onto the stage, chanting and changing the scene. Flora remains seated, quietly folding the letter.*)

[MUSIC #16b *"WINDS" WITH CHANT*]

ALL.
WAGES UP, HOURS DOWN
MAKE NEW YORK A UNION TOWN

WAGES UP, HOURS DOWN
MAKE NEW YORK A UNION TOWN

WAGES UP, HOURS DOWN
MAKE NEW YORK A UNION TOWN

WAGES UP, HOURS DOWN
MAKE NEW YORK A UNION TOWN

(*The strikers exit. Flora is alone. On another part of the stage, a light comes up on Willy who sings.*)

[MUSIC #16c *"QUIET THING" REPRISE*]

REPRISE: QUIET THING

WILLY.
WHEN IT ALL COMES TRUE
JUST THE WAY YOU PLANNED
IT'S FUNNY BUT THE BELLS DON'T RING
IT'S A QUIET THING

(*During the song, a spotlight hits Kenny and Maggie as they come onto the stage. We see them at their audition — excited and full of hope. They smile, bow slightly and — in slow motion — begin to do part of their routine*)

WHEN YOU HOLD THE WORLD
IN YOUR TREMBLING HAND

(*Slowly, Flora gets up from the chair and exits.*)

YOU'D THINK YOU'D HEAR A CHOIR SING
IT'S A QUIET THING

(*The lights crossfade as the music segues to "Keepin' It Hot." We are now in the studio and Kenny and Maggie finish their routine for Mr. Weiss, Willy and Elsa.*)

SCENE SEVEN

The Studio
WILLY. So? So?

KENNY. So we're holding this position.

MAGGIE. There's dead silence.

KENNY. (*As if bad news is going to follow.*) We break the pose and the manager is just staring at us.

MAGGIE. The ash on his cigar is about this long—

KENNY. The ash drops—(*they both watch an imaginary ash fall*)—and he says:

MAGGIE. (*Dryly. Without compassion.*) "You're hired." (*An electric shock jolts through everyone and they jump and scream.*) Just like that! Ten weeks as part of the floor show.

WILLY. I knew it!

ELSA. It was the lace.

WILLY. The music!

MAGGIE. It was everything!

MR. WEISS. Well come on! We have to celebrate!

KENNY. Let's go next door for a drink. It's on us!

WILLY. (*Everyone agrees and begins to get their coats.*) I'll vote for that!

(*Flora enters.*)

MAGGIE. Flora!

KENNY. We got the job!

FLORA. I knew it! Congratulations!

MAGGIE. You would have been so proud of us.

KENNY. It went beautifully.

MAGGIE. It's all because you got us an audition.

KENNY. We'll buy you that fur yet—stick with us.

FLORA. It's a deal!

ELSA. Come on—enough of this—the celebration awaits.

KENNY. Come on Flora! (*As they exit.*)

FLORA. I'll be along in a few minutes. I've got a few things to do.

WILLY. Okay—but don't be too long.

KENNY. Then let's go. (*They exit.*)

MR. WEISS. (*Who has stayed behind.*) Everything work out at the store?

FLORA. Fine. Just fine.

MR. WEISS. You crossed the picket line, didn't you?

FLORA. Yes.

MR. WEISS. That doesn't put you in very good standing with the party, does it.

FLORA. Doesn't put me in any standing.

MR. WEISS. Of course, you could apologize to the Disciplinary Committee.

FLORA. (*Determined.*) No. I won't do that.

MR. WEISS. And what about the store?

FLORA. Mr. Weiss . . . I lost my job.

MR. WEISS. I'm sorry. Did anyone else on the list?

FLORA. No.

MR. WEISS. No? First sign of a union and they usually clean shop! You must have thought very fast on your feet.

FLORA. You know me—I can think fast.

MR. WEISS. Yes you can. (*Then.*) So what about Harry?

FLORA. I don't know. But if two people really care about each other—then there's always everything to hope for. Right?

MR. WEISS. (*Kindly.*) That's right.

(*Harry enters.*)

FLORA. Hello Harry.

MR. WEISS. Harry.

HARRY. Mr. Weiss.

MR. WEISS. I'll see you downstairs.

HARRY. I just wanted to make sure everything got straightened out at the store.

FLORA. Well, it depends on who you ask.

HARRY. But no one lost their jobs?

FLORA. No. (*Then.*) No one.

HARRY. L-look, Flora—

FLORA. Harry—I want to say—(*then*)—go ahead.

HARRY. It's not going to work out.

FLORA. Oh Harry—no. How can you say that?

HARRY. I mean, you'd never be committed to the party. Not the way I am. You'd say you were b-but you'd only be s-saying it because of me. And that's not good enough. You have to f-feel it. Here. You'd only be lying if you didn't.

FLORA. Aw Harry—

HARRY. F-Flora, you approach things exactly the way you feel about them. You can't hide anything. You c-can't help it.

FLORA. I know. Sometimes I get in the way of myself. I could change that.

HARRY. And wh-what good would that do anyone. Flora—

you have g-given me so much. My art. The confidence to s-speak.
So many things. It's because of you I f-feel I can do more.

FLORA. Then why can't we be together?

HARRY. Because — because I've got this crazy idea to change
the world.

FLORA. So do I!

HARRY. But we g-go about it in different ways. Together —
you'd be pushing. I'd be pulling. And you know what? We'd
never get anywhere. (*Then.*) We don't have time for that.

FLORA. Well, Harry — will you stay here? In the studio? I
mean —

HARRY. L-look — it was worked out so that I could share the
studio with the artists at the Daily Worker.

FLORA. Oh.

HARRY. Yeah — I'll be able to work on a lot of party materials
—and the s-space is free . . . so . . .

FLORA. So you'll be able to finish your mural there, won't you?

HARRY. I've already s-started a new one.

FLORA. So I guess this means no more apples.

HARRY. (*He gives her one last apple.*) No more apples. (*There
is an awkward moment.*) Would it be okay if I picked up my
things later . . . some p-people are waiting for me.

FLORA. Sure. (*She moves toward him. He puts his hand out.
She puts her arms around him. They embrace. Harry leaves. She
is left alone in the studio.*)

[MUSIC #17: *SING HAPPY*]

FLORA.
ALL I NEED IS ONE GOOD BREAK, JUST ONE . . .

(*Looking at the apple, she sits. And through her tears, she sings.*)

SING ME A HAPPY SONG ABOUT ROBINS IN SPRING
SING ME A HAPPY SONG WITH A HAPPY ENDING
SOME CHEERFUL RONDELAY ABOUT CATCHING
   THE RING
SING HAPPY

SING ME A SONNET ALL ABOUT ROLLING IN GOLD

SOME PEPPY MELODY ABOUT RAINBOWS BLENDING
NOTHING WITH PHRASES SAYING YOU'RE OUT IN
  THE COLD
SING HAPPY

TELL ME TOMORROW'S GONNA BE PEACHES AND
  CREAM
ASSURE ME CLOUDS ARE LINED WITH A SILVER
  LINING
SAY HOW YOU REALIZE AN IMPOSSIBLE DREAM
SING ME A HAPPY SONG

PLAY ME A MADRIGAL ABOUT TRIPS TO THE MOON
OR SOME OLD BALLAD ALL ABOUT TWO EYES
  SHINING
IT CAN'T BE LOUD ENOUGH OR A MOMENT TOO SOON
SING HAPPY

NO NEED REMINDING ME HOW IT ALL FELL APART
I NEED NO LYRIC SINGING OF STORMY WEATHER
THERE'S QUITE ENOUGH AROUND ME THAT'S
  BREAKING MY HEART
SING HAPPY

GIVE ME A HALLELUJAH AND GET UP AND SHOUT
TELL ME THE SUN IS SHINING AROUND THE CORNER
WHOEVER'S INTERESTED IN HELPING ME OUT
PLEASE KEEP IT HAPPY

I'M ONLY IN THE MARKET FOR LONG, LOUD
  LAUGHTER
I'LL LET YOU SERENADE ME TILL DAWN COMES
  ALONG
JUST MAKE IT A HAPPY
KEEP IT A HAPPY
SONG!

WILLY. (*He enters.*) Hey—do you need anything?

FLORA. Oh—

WILLY. We're all downstairs. Waiting for you. Not much of a celebration without you. How about it? A cup of coffee? It's a beautiful night out there. What do you say?

FLORA. Well—

WILLY. (*Playfully imitating her.*) Well—

FLORA. Okay . . .

WILLY. Okay?

FLORA. Okay yes.

WILLY. Okay yes! Good. Here's your coat. In fact—it's just started to snow out there.

FLORA. Thanks Willy. (*She hugs him.*)

WILLY. Sure! We gotta take care of our Flora, huh? Now come on, let's go. I'll get the lights. (*Flora exits. Willy turns and directly addresses the audience.*) She's gonna be all right. Things are going to get better. I really think so. Well, that's our story. Thanks for coming. (*Then.*) Remember us. Good night.

[MUSIC #18 *BOWS*]

PROP LIST

ACT ONE

1-1:   radio

1-2:   telephone
8 job applications
12 pencils
3 small portfolios, 3 sketch samples (artists)
portfolio and small red book (H)
carpetbag, sketch sample (F)
steno pad, white notebook (M)
dress in large box (E)

1-3:   2 apples (MW)
nickel (H)
carpetbag, white, bloodied hankie (F) (from 1-2)
small book, portfolio (H) (from 1-2)
brown shopping bag with remnants and purple dress (E)
clarinet and case (W)
pocketwatch, jeweler's lupe, screwdriver (MW)

1-4:   carpetbag, hankie (F) (from 1-2)
portfolio (H) (from 1-2)
ice in hankie (W)

1-5:   carpetbag, bread pieces, cheese puffs, cheese sticks,
towel (F) Communist Party application, small/blunt pencil (H)

1-6:   clarinet (W) (from 1-3)
small piece of paper (W)
dress maker's dummy, purple dress (E)
pocketwatch, polishing cloth (MW) (from 1-3)

1-7:   dress in box (M)
telephone, file folder with papers, pencil, sketch sample
(S) carpet bag, coat (F)

1-8:   red scarf (C)
gavel, agenda papers (MW)
white flyers (E)
bag of marbles, carpetbag, G&M box (F)

1-9:   sketchpad, pencils, carpet bag
white shopping bag and large box (F)

purple flyers, apple (H)

1-10:   newspaper — single sheet (MW)
carpetbag, sketch sample, sketchpad (F)
4 white boxes with blue ribbon and bows (K)
file folder, sketch sample (S)
steno pad, pencil (M)
elevator bell (on piano)

1-11:   sketchpad, pencil, carpetbag (F)
Valentine's box of candy
red scarf (H)
wilted daisy (H)

ACT TWO

2-1:   clarinet (W)

2-2:   blanket
red scarf (C)
bag of marbles (H)
candy box (F)

2-3:   makeshift baby with purple towel (M)
yellow ric rac (E)
small box of trim, carpetbag, blue Garret and Mellick's
envelope
clarinet (W)
8×11 speech, sunglasses (C)
large sketch pad, pencil (H)

2-4:   pencil, sample sketch with tissue cover (F)
2 blue Garret and Mellick envelopes, list of 33 names,
carpetbag (F)
tux box with white dinner jacket (W)
dollar bill — cab fare (F)
rhinestone earrings (MW)

2-5:   piece of paper — speech, scarf (H)
bag of marbles (H)
4 picket signs — WORKERS UNITED (H)
STRIKE (E)
STRIKE FOR BETTER WAGES (W)
(MW)
carpetbag (F)

2-6:   telephone
       33 letters (M)
       folded newspaper, pencil, blue Garret and Mellick enve-
       lope with list of 33 names (S)

2-8:   carpet bag (F)
       apple (H)

KEY:
(F)—Flora
(H)—Harry
(W)—Willy
(C)—Charlotte
(M)—Maggie
(K)—Kenny
(S)—Mr. Stanley
(MW)—Mr. Weiss
(E)—Elsa

COSTUMES
This is a production of the WPA and the costumes should be
simple and look like street clothes from 1935. With the exception
of Flora, Harry and Charlotte, the actors play many different
characters and a different look is needed for each. Sometimes
simple accessories—hats, coats or jackets—are enough. Other
times, a more complete costume change is necessary.

FLORA
Throughout the entire show, Flora's basic costume is a robins-egg
blue dress. She should look a little off-beat . . . slightly off-
center. After all, she is an artist. At various times, she wears a
cloth winter coat and muffler. She also needs a cap and gown, a
spectacular fur coat, a stunning beaded floor-length gown (which
is also worn by Elsa) a "Chinese-style" day dress which fits very
snuggly at the knees (making it nearly impossible to walk) and
which rips—on cue—up the back.

CHARLOTTE
Black crepe pants, belted tunic, camisole, cloth winter coat and
long red muffler
PROLOGUE: Cloth coat and later, cap and gown

HARRY
Grey pants with suspenders, white shirt, maroon cardigan, cloth winter coat, black cap and later, red muffler like Charlotte's
PROLOGUE: cloth coat and later, cap and gown

WILLY
Burgandy vest and tan cardigan, blue shirt, brown pants, short blue jacket, muffler and cap
PROLOGUE: Argyle sweater, tie, cap and gown
ARTIST: Removes sweater
COMMUNIST: Burgandy sweater and eye glasses, dark grey overcoat and fedora
ELEVATOR OPERATOR: Blue Garret and Mellick smock

MR. WEISS
Brown suit with white shirt and maroon bow tie, striped sweater vest, brown overcoat and fedora
PROLOGUE: Heavy brown cardigan and cap and later, cap and gown
APPLE SELLER: Black overcoat and cap
COMMUNIST: Maroon overshirt, dark brown coat and cap

KENNY
Blue flannel pants, red suspenders, grey striped shirt, tweed coat and grey fedora
Rehearses in a t-shirt
White dinner jacket with tuxedo pants, shirt
PROLOGUE: Grey pants, stripped shirt, tie, overcoat and fedora and later, cap and gown.
ARTIST: Removes coat
COMMUNIST: Grey pants, stripped shirt, glasses, dark grey coat and muffler

MR. STANLEY
Blue pin-stripe suit, navy and grey stripped tie and tie tac
PROLOGUE: Blue tweed overcoat and fedora and later, cap and gown
ARTIST: "Mr. Stanley" outfit minus coat
COMMUNIST: Navy applejack, navy sweater and cap, blue tweed overcoat

ELSA
Violet flowered dress, purple sweater, purple overcoat and black-trimmed hat
(She also poses for Flora wearing the beaded full-length gown.)
PROLOGUE: Brown tweed coat, hat and cut-off gloves over orange dress and later cap and gown.
STORE RUNNER: Blue Garret and Mellick's smock
COMMUNIST: Navy blue dress and blue sweater, tan overcoat, muffler and gloves

MAGGIE
Peach dress, peach sweater, tan overcoat, muffler and gloves
Silver audition dress and shoes
PROLOGUE: Cranberry dress, jacket, hat and gloves and later, cap and gown.
MISS WILLIAMS: Red white and blue polka dotted dress and shoes
COMMUNIST: Burgandy dress and sweater, scarf, open-toed orthos and ankle stockings, glasses and a needle-point hoop with Communist insignia which is later used like a tambourine in THE FLAME.
Burgandy overcoat, hat and gloves

PIANO PLAYER
If the piano player is in view of the audience, he or she should wear a simple outfit from the period.

NOTE:
Magggie, like many of the characters, is a study in quick changes and many of the outfits must be worn under other costumes and coats.

Lightning Source UK Ltd.
Milton Keynes UK
UKHW021548191118
332604UK00005B/188/P